# The Unicorn's Tale

# The Unicorn's Tale

By David Franklin

Synaptic
Firestorm

"The King Prepares to Mount His Noble Steed" Copyright © 1192 by Heathrow Payne & Co.

ISBN-13: 978-1502832528
ISBN-10: 1502832526

*For Jessi, who brings wind chimes and
laughter—with endless sparkles thrown in.*

The following is based on an actual story, though not
necessarily a *true* actual story. Some parts of it are true and some I
have made up in the hopes of creating a book interesting enough
for people to want to buy. Which parts are which, I'll leave for you,
Dear Reader, to decide for yourself, beginning with this paragraph.

Any similarities between this story and actual Unicorns
currently living in Europe and owned by farm girls named
Amethyst are entirely coincidental.

# Contents

Unicorns are believed by most people to be extinct or the products of children's imaginations. In this first point, most people are wrong, and in this second point...well, you will see.

It has been suggested by some of the more learned people among us, who have usually also been some of the more serious people among us, that unicorns never existed in the flesh, and that they are merely legends inspired by other animals that have a single horn. That's an understandable mistake, given the similarities between unicorns and other single-horned animals; the differences can sometimes be hard to detect.

For example, see if you can identify the differences in the following pictures:

*Unicorn*

*Not a Unicorn*

Were you able to spot the difference? That's right; the unicorn has *purple* eyes. Nice catch for someone inexperienced enough not to skip over a section called "On the Methods and Manners of Unicorns."

Other people have suggested that unicorns may have existed before the great flood of Noah in the Bible, but that the unicorns that were chosen to have ridden the waves in Noah's Ark were in fact delayed by an especially tasty-looking patch of wild strawberries and therefore missed the boat, ending forever the graceful and noble line of the fore-horned. This suggestion is also wrong, as there were in fact two nearly perfect unicorns, Tycra and his mate Gensella, on the Ark, and they have been overlooked in the story for millennia largely because they (unlike the monkeys, who might have been tossed overboard had Noah been able to catch them up in the rafters) were so well behaved that they never caused a moment's trouble for Noah or his family, and were therefore never mentioned in the story at all. And so it was the line of unicorns was saved and that every unicorn down to the present day is descended from the nearly perfect lineage of Tycra and Gensella.

By the Middle Ages[*] it was widely believed that having a unicorn at the lead of an army meant almost certain victory. This is also wrong. That bit of malarkey arose from two characteristics of unicorns.

The first characteristic is that unicorns hardly ever reproduce. This meant that throughout the age of castles and kings there were precious few unicorns about at any given moment. This made verifiable unicorn sightings exceedingly rare. In fact, sightings were so rare that most people came to believe that the noble beasts existed only in legends, like the Loch Ness Monster or honest politicians, and weren't real at all. Naturally, that being the age of fairytales, the simple people of that time assumed if any such

---

[*] It may be useful at this juncture to point out that they didn't call it the Middle Ages back then because there hadn't been any ages after it yet to make it the Middle Ages. They most often referred to it as the "Exceedingly Recent Ages" (which has since been shortened to our modern word "era") or, more simply, "yesterday."

mystical creatures did exist, they must surely have tremendous magical powers (the unicorns, not the politicians).

The second characteristic is that unicorns have tremendous magical powers. These powers, however, did not usually help one army to defeat another since unicorns are decidedly against people deliberately hurting each other unless one side is especially Good and the other side is especially Evil. Only in such cases would a unicorn, like the Swiss army, make an exception to its policy of strict neutrality.

Though these delicate creatures (unicorns, not the Swiss army) were not well suited to pulling plows or wagons, they would, on a good day, have little trouble carrying a king in full battle armor. Most people who were not kings, however, and were not consumed by thoughts of wars and weaponry, would never think of putting a saddle on such a lithe and beautiful creature (again, the unicorn, not the king). It was true, however, that, aside from the presence of the horn and a general impression of *betterness* that unicorns cast, they very closely resembled the common farm horse.

This fact was not overlooked by King Pliny the Wiley who, in an effort to secure victory for castle and country, attempted to intimidate an opposing army by strapping a fake horn onto the forehead of his draft horse, Feldspar. Regrettably, the fake horn began to loosen in the heat of battle until it had slipped badly and was mounted to the side of the horse's head like one handlebar of a bicycle. The valiant and clever—though ridiculous looking at this point, with a fake horn protruding from the side of his head—the valiant and clever horse turned his head sharply to avoid a blow from an enemy. The move was a very good one for Feldspar—for he avoided a well-aimed blow from a large and dangerous foe—but a very bad one for Pliny, who ended up being stabbed in the shoulder with the fake horn, knocked to the ground, and as a result lost the battle and his kingdom. Thus, with one swift motion of a horse's head, did Pliny lose his kingdom and have his name changed to Pliny the Unfortunate.

Although unicorns are among the most blessed of the four-footed, they do not multiply readily or often. They, like people, must have three things to thrive: food, safety, love, and strawberries (okay, that's four things). Horses are herd animals; they crave the company of other horses. Unicorns, being a higher species, require something more: a deep soul connection with a human being. Without it, they're as incomplete as a barbarian without his battleaxe.

Once established, this connection between human and beast will grow and strengthen over time like a young tree growing in its connection with the earth. This continues until breaking the connection would be...well, it wouldn't be pretty, you can bet the farm on that. The connection affects both the human and the unicorn, though it affects the fore-horn more deeply, and in more obvious ways. This is why a unicorn will not attach strongly to an evil person, and, if it has begun to do so in error, it will break the connection and seek out a purer heart to love. The breaking of the connection can be quite traumatic for the unicorn, especially if the connection was allowed to grow for a time before the unicorn discovered the true nature of the one he or she had chosen.

Though their nobility shines brightest when defending or nurturing their humans, unicorns are tender and tremulous animals when alone. This has long been a source of great difficulty for the beautiful creatures. They have such slight constitution and such advanced intelligence that putting them to work is usually out of the question. The reason for this is simple: they were created to serve a different function than their plow-horse or war-horse cousins. Because they were not suited for such uses as a farmer would need, and preferred to eat grain (and strawberries—have I mentioned the strawberries?) that would otherwise go toward feeding animals that "pulled their weight" on a farm, unicorns were turned out into the forests to fend for themselves. Over time, their difficulty surviving without close human contact, and their exceptionally polite behavior, caused the unicorn to all but disappear from human experience.

Removing a unicorn's horn can be painful for the 'corn, especially if it is cut too close to the head. The horn will grow back, however, sometimes at an incredible rate (you don't want to be standing in the way), once the creature has established the required trust relationship with its human.

So ends the introductory background information. Thank you for your attention. Now, on to the story....

# Amethyst and Her Mother

Once Upon a Time, long ago and far away in a mythical land called Europe, lay the Royal Kingdom of Rondolay. Near the center of the kingdom, slightly off to one side, stood a beautiful castle with colored banners waving happily from the tip of each of its many gleaming spires. In the castle lived an even-tempered princess named Gwyneth with her sour-faced and somewhat annoying little brother, Prince Todd. Neither Gwyneth nor her brother possessed much imagination. They never had any adventures, nor even any personal goals or plans for self-improvement. As a result, their days were mostly spent on whatever Royalty Training Activities their father, who was the king—though not a particularly noble or wise king—decided they should do. When Gwyneth was not preening through the beautifully colored dresses that filled her Royal Wardrobe, she was engaged in activities like learning to walk with a book balanced on her head and learning to stick out her pinky when she drank tea. Todd, likewise, followed his Renaissance Behavioral Coach around all day, learning to speak using "thou" and "thee," and how to look menacing on horseback.

All in all, they were not a terribly interesting pair of children.

This story is not about them.

* * *

Just over three miles from the castle stood—
leaned, really—a little stone farmhouse. It had a
thatched roof and so much moss growing on the
stone walls that, if its occupants had taken to
scraping any of it off, the place would undoubtedly have fallen in ruins. There was a pleasant
curl of smoke stretching lazily from the vine-
covered chimney. Outside the wooden plank
door was a little yard where a young girl named
Amethyst had just finished hanging some tattered
laundry. The entire scene smelled strongly of
boiled rhubarb.

"Aaaaaaaaaaaaa-chooooo!!!!"

Amethyst was an orderly, punctual, and
allergic child who spent her days working
alongside her mother, trying to scrape a living
from the barren, desolate rock pile they called the
family farm. It was withering work, but Amethyst
and her mother didn't complain for two reasons:
first, it didn't do any good to complain and,
second, they couldn't spare the time. Amethyst's
days had been filled with work since that foggy
night when her father had pushed back from the
supper table, picked up a wooden milking pail,
and opened the front door, announcing, "Back
shortly. Going for some milk." He had headed
for the dilapidated barn where Petunia, the
emaciated family cow, was bellowing to be
milked. Unfortunately, Amethyst's father was
even worse with direction than he was at selecting
prime farm land, so it hadn't come as a complete

17

surprise when he never returned. Amethyst's mother had always feared it would happen, even though the barn was only 60 feet from the house. In the two long years since that night, Amethyst and her mother hadn't received the slightest word of his—

"Aaaaaaaaaaaaa-chooooo!!!!"

Amethyst left the laundry line and retrieved Petunia from where she was standing nearly comatose in the flower bed beside the house. The old cow was chewing incessantly, occasionally dipping her head and gingerly working her mouth around the industrial-strength thistles that had decisively conquered the begonias. Amethyst led the cow into the barn and put her into the stall next to Massey Fergusson, their aged and boney plow-horse. Amethyst set the two-legged milking stool next to Petunia and began milking. It didn't take long.

The barn was ancient, built of stone and thick wooden beams. It had moss growing between the stones, and mouse holes in the wood because Clawed, the Laziest Cat in the World, had never developed any serious ambitions as a mouser—or anything else, for that matter. He was so lazy, in fact, that the family had once mistakenly thought him dead and tried to bury him. Amethyst's father had just tossed the first shovelful of dirt on him when an annoyed "*eeeeooow*" was heard from the bottom of the hole, and they realized that Clawed had not yet departed for the great scratching post in the sky.

Amethyst sometimes wondered what would have happened if, instead of burying him, they had attempted to have the cat stuffed.

Amethyst finished milking and headed back to the house.

"Aaaaaaaaaaaaa-chooooo!!!!" she blasted as she passed through the doorway into the cramped room that served as their kitchen/bedroom/dinette.

"Gracious!" exclaimed Amethyst's startled mother, bending to pick up the rhubarb she had dropped. "Such a noise from one so small!" Truly, it was an impressive quantity of sound from the eight-year old—but then again, she'd been practicing for years. In the nearby town and surrounding countryside, Amethyst's sinuses were the stuff of legend.

Amethyst beamed as she held up two thimbles full of milk. "Look, Mother!" she said. "We got twice the usual amount!"

"Oh, blessed be!" sang Amethyst's mother. "We'll enjoy that after supper tonight—if we have any. In the meantime, take this rhubarb to town and sell it to the peasants."

Now, when Amethyst's mother used the term "peasants," she meant it with the highest possible respect, for she and Amethyst would need to move up two full social classes (right past "street beggars") to gain entry into the privileged and opulent ranks of Rondolay's lowly peasants. Amethyst dreamed of becoming a peasant one day; she had even entered it as one of her Life

Goals in her *Knight-Timer Personal Planner.*

Amethyst poured the milk into a cracked teacup, then lifted the small basket of limp rhubarb stalks—

Since rhubarb isn't nearly as popular today as it was at one point in history, and since it was never all that popular even then, this might be a good time to provide some additional background information:

# On the Methods and Manners of Rhubarb

*Rheum rhabarbarum,* or "rhubarb," is a plant that has enjoyed limited success as food because it is poisonous.[†] The rhubarb plant consists of a potato-like bulb that sits in the ground and year after year sprouts stalks that are just like celery except for being inedibly tough, eye-stingingly sour, and red. The stalks are topped by poisonous leaves.

If rhubarb stalks are boiled for a long time, they soften up to the point that they can be eaten by humans without dying, though they are still so sour (the stalks, not the people) that it's like drinking lemonade from which the "ade" has been removed.

Rhubarb's principle use throughout the ages has been as a socially acceptable way to consume vast quantities of sugar, particularly in pies. A long time ago somebody noticed that a tart flavor mixed with a sweet flavor and wrapped in a pie crust can be very tasty. In the case of rhubarb pie, people mix loads of sugar with boiled, hammered rhubarb stalks to achieve this flavor experience. It's the same idea as cherry pie except people actually like to eat cherries. The pinnacle of rhubarb's cultural importance came with the invention of the strawberry-rhubarb pie.

---

[†] It's true. Look it up if you don't believe me.

Since rhubarb is almost the same color as cooked strawberries, a strawberry-rhubarb pie is a convenient place to hide rhubarb if someone gives you some and you don't know what else to do with it, provided you don't put in enough of the stalks to ruin the pie or enough of the leaves to ruin your friends.

At certain times in history rhubarb has been used in medicines despite having no medicinal value whatsoever. This came about when some people noticed that things we love to eat are often very unhealthy, and so assumed that the opposite should also hold true. This resulted in generations of parents going about forcing their children to swallow things like rhubarb, cod liver oil, and various petroleum products, reasoning that anything people hate that intensely must surely be good for them. Those people are all dead now.

People disagree about whether rhubarb is a fruit or a vegetable. It looks like a vegetable, and grows like a vegetable, but a New York court ruled in 1947 that it could be a fruit since it was used in pies (establishing an early precedent of denying reality, a policy New York courts have followed ever since). To this day, the controversy of whether rhubarb is a fruit or a vegetable has yet to be finally settled, mostly because no one cares either way.

Before he disappeared, Amethyst's father, being the keen visionary that he was, had believed there was great potential for the underappreciated plant, despite it being poisonous. He was convinced a great rhubarb craze lay just around the corner, and therefore converted the family farm to 100% rhubarb production so he would be able to corner the market of the up-and-coming rhubarb industry when it arrived.

Amethyst and her mother are still waiting for the promised rhubarb mania as we rejoin them in the kitchen/bedroom/dinette conversation, already in progress:

Amethyst poured the milk into a cracked teacup, then lifted the small basket of limp rhubarb stalks and hooked it over her arm.

"Remember to look mournful so they will feel sorry for you and pay a higher price," said Amethyst's mother. "Let me see mournful."

Amethyst made a sad face.

"Ugh!" said her mother. "You want to scare away the peasants? Maybe you'd better try for plaintive. Show me plaintive."

Amethyst made a sad face.

"Much better," said her mother. "You practice that on your way into town. Now, off with you, and don't be late for supper, if we have any!"

Amethyst set off across the dusty yard, past the field of withered rhubarb, and out onto the rutted wagon road, skipping merrily as she went. She worked so hard at her plaintive expression that she was easily the saddest looking girl ever to skip merrily down a country road. The trees that hung over the road were old and sturdy, and threw down large splotches of shade that

Amethyst found refreshing (*aaaaaaaaaaaaa-chooooo!!!!*) She was skipping from shadow to shadow, trying to see how far she could go without touching any sunlit spots—

—when she suddenly heard a sound unlike anything she had ever heard before. It sounded like an animal, but...musical. It was as if a horse's whinny had been mixed with wind chimes and children laughing, and been released on the morning breeze. Amethyst stopped abruptly and cupped her unbasketed hand behind her ear.

"Hark!" she said. "What in the world can that be?" She looked across a field toward the source of the sound.

And there it was.

There, at the crest of a perfectly symmetrical hill, illuminated by rays of sunlight streaming through the clouds as if centered in heaven's attention, in the middle of a patch of wild strawberries, stood...

...a tree stump.

It wasn't much as tree stumps go, all cracked and weathered with some fungus growing on the north side, well on its way to becoming one with the earth.

But next to the stump stood a baby horse.

Now, those who know about such things will immediately interject, "You mean 'a foal,' Mr. Narrator," to which I say you're right, I do mean 'a foal,' but as I'm trying to be as optimistic as possible about the readership of this story, and since it's just possible that some of those readers might not know that a foal is a baby horse, and since this is one of the two or three most important parts of the story, I didn't want those unhorsed readers to hit that 'foal' word and scratch their collective head and think, "I wonder what he means by *that?*" and have one of the two or three most important parts of the story happen while they're in the attic shuffling through stacks of their mother's old college books looking for a dictionary, all because they have never in their lives been horseback riding. So there.

Anyway, as I was saying...

There, at the crest of a perfectly symmetrical hill yaddah, yaddah, yaddah, tree stump, blah, blah, blah...stood a baby horse. It was an exquisite, delicate, adorable little thing, with slender legs that reached all the way to the ground. It looked to be maybe two months old, and Amethyst was struck by an odd mixture of impressions: the animal seemed frail yet majestic, dainty yet fierce. It was the whitest of whites all over, except for a red dribble of strawberry juice on its chin. The foal (remember that means "baby horse") locked eyes with Amethyst and whinnied that nickering/wind chime/laughter sound again, this time with some sparkles thrown in.

Amethyst replied with her most friendly sneeze. "Well, hello to you, too," she said.

It was odd that the little creature (the horse, not Amethyst) wasn't tied or fenced at all. In fact, there were no other farms around for miles. It was as free as a dandelion puff skipping across a wildflower meadow. Amethyst knew she must get to town in case there was a sudden run on pre-wilted rhubarb, but something in the shimmering foal's gaze wouldn't let her go. What if she could catch it? Massey Fergusson was old and worn from years of pulling a plow. They were going to need a replacement soon. But Amethyst knew she could never catch a horse—even one this young—unless it wanted to be caught. She held out a fistful of rhubarb from her basket and started toward the foal.

"Come on now....That's it....That's a good boy."

The white foal didn't move. Even this young, the animal had an air of pride and competence about it (though what a baby horse would have to feel competent about, I don't know). It just stood like stone, watching Amethyst's advance.

Staring...staring...

Closer...closer...

Staring.

Closer.

Pride.

*Competence.*

Amethyst reached the animal and held forth the rhubarb stalks like a bouquet of flowers without the flower parts. The foal eyed the rhubarb (staring) then raised one eyebrow as if to say, "You want me to eat *that?*" The foal cautiously sniffed the offering (rhubarb), then nibbled a bit.

Chewing.

Chewing.

The other eyebrow went up as if to say, "Not bad, kid. Not bad at all."

Amethyst took a step backward, keeping the rhubarb just out of the animal's reach.

The foal took a step forward.

Amethyst rewarded him with a rhubarb stalk, then took two steps back.

The foal took two steps forward.

Back.

Forward.

Chew.

Back.

Forward.

Chew—

You get the idea.

27

Her basket was nearly empty as they arrived at the lane that led to Amethyst's barn.

"Mother! Mother!" she called. "Come see what I have found!"

Her mother appeared at the plank door, wiping her hands on the part of her skirt she used as a dishrag. When she saw the little horse her face bloomed into surprised joy.

"Oh, well done, Amethyst! Wherever did you find him? Looks like we'll be having supper after all!"

"Mother!" Amethyst looked shocked. "Perish the thought! I brought him home so he can grow up big and strong and replace Massey Fergusson someday. We have room for him in the barn. I'll muck out his stall and I promise I'll feed him every day. Can we keep him, Mother, pleeeeeeeeease?" Amethyst had switched to a whiny sort of voice that you almost never hear from the well behaved heroines of fairytales.

"Surely he belongs to someone."

"I found him in the big strawberry patch along the road into town. He was roaming around loose, and there was no one in sight."

"Well, I don't know...," said Amethyst's mother. "You know we barely have enough hay for ourselves. What would he eat?"

"Well," Amethyst offered sheepishly, "he loves rhubarb."

"Rhubarb!" Amethyst's mother said in surprise. "Rhubarb?" She looked thoughtful.

Amethyst saw it was a look with real possibilities. "Rhubarb...."

"Pleeeeeeeeeease." Amethyst gave her a plaintive look. The practicing paid off.

"All right," said Amethyst's mother. "I do not suppose it shall hurt to keep him around a little while to see if he might be of some use. Besides, it will be nice to have someone around who actually wants our rhubarb."

"Hoo-ah!" Amethyst pumped her fist in the air. She fed the white foal another rhubarb stalk.

"Don't feed him too much. If we don't get some rain soon, I'm afraid we'll lose the rhubarb crop and there won't be anything to eat at all."

When Amethyst's mother said this, the white foal's ears suddenly darted forward, and a strange look clouded his eyes. It was almost as if he had understood her words, if such a thing were possible for a horse.

As was their habit, Amethyst and her mother didn't notice.

"What will you name him, Amethyst?"

"I'm going to call him Nova."

"Nova?" said Amethyst's mother. "You mean like an exploding star?"

"Oh, Mother, what an imagination you have!" said Amethyst. "No, not like an exploding star. You see, 'Nova' is Spanish for 'it doesn't go,' and I never want him to go away."

"I understand how you feel, but we'll have to sell him if it doesn't work out."

"Oh, he'll work out," said Amethyst,

leading him toward the barn. "I'll put him in the barn with Massey Fergusson. By the way, Mother, what's for supper—if we're having any?"

The next morning Amethyst arose at dawn, and prepared to go care for the animals. As she left the house she found the farmyard filled with a thick fog, as if a cloud had grown tired of floating around and had settled on their farm for a rest. It wasn't damp enough to make the ground muddy, but Amethyst noticed the leaves of the rhubarb plants were shiny with wetness. She knew her mother would be glad for the moisture, but Amethyst felt a tinge of uneasiness: you could lose relatives in a fog like this.

As she opened the barn door, she wondered if Petunia would give enough milk to—

She stopped.

Massey Fergusson was standing—sort of—with his rump up in the air, kneeling on his knobby forelegs with his nose just touching the dirt floor. He was pointed toward Nova, who was peeking out between the boards of his stall. Amethyst had the absurd impression that the old plow-puller was *bowing* to the white foal.

"My goodness, Massey Fergusson, what are you doing?" said Amethyst.

The old horse struggled to his hooves, looking slightly embarrassed, if such a thing is possible for a horse.

Amethyst thought it strange for a moment, but, being the heroine in a fairytale, wasn't

30

majorly affected by things any normal person would find truly bizarre. She pulled some rhubarb from her basket and began feeding Nova.

Petunia the cow gave a whole cup of milk that morning.

Three miles away in the center of the town, King Engelbert was in his castle having his regular Saturday morning Council of War with his Noblemen. In the center of the room was a long, rectangular table covered with hand-drawn maps. Long, intricate tapestries covered the walls, many of which had been embroidered by the king's wife, Queen Arabella, during her "indoor fineries" phase. A fire blazed at one end of the room in an ornate fireplace that was roughly the size of a Zamboni.

King Engelbert was dressed in his Royal Bathrobe and fur-lined slippers, sitting with one leg flopped over the arm of a hand-carved chair that was smaller than his Royal Throne, but obviously bigger than any of the other chairs in the room. He was biting his fingernails like a gerbil trying to chew its way to oxygen.

Periodically, King Engelbert would pause in his nail biting and glance at his reflection in a wall-mounted mirror. Most people who spent any time with him believed this habit of his to be the result of a misplaced (some said *extremely* misplaced) fondness for his own image. After all, they said, there was at least one mirror in every room of the castle. But it was not a love of the way he looked that kept the king checking his reflection, but a fear of it. In reality, when those near him thought he was admiring his kingly features, he was in actuality verifying the position of the Royal Hairpiece.

You see, King Engelbert suffered from *alopecia*, a rare condition which causes, to a greater or lesser degree, one's hair to come loose. The king, unfortunately, had a Royal Case of the disorder, and so from the top of his head to the bottoms of his feet, he was as hairless as a freshly shaved bowling ball. I mean he had no hair at all: no eyebrows, no chest hair, no leg hair. This was a source of great embarrassment for him, for he believed people would laugh at him if they knew, and, even though he was the king, he didn't like to be laughed at any more than you or I do. As a result, King Engelbert's life was a study in the art and usage of artificial hair: fake eyebrows, false mustaches, and a rabbit pelt for his chest hair. He would sometimes stand before his dressing room mirror admiring the way he looked with a swath of rabbit pelt stuffed down the front of his tunic, intended to simulate Royal Chest Hair. He thought he looked quite manly. The Nobles thought he looked like he had a weasel hiding in his shirt.

On this particular Saturday morning, King Engelbert had been trying something new to keep the Royal Hairpiece in place: a sticky derivative of pine sap that he painted onto the top of his head with a horsehair brush. The first version of the formula had been too thick and had resulted only in gluing the horsehair brush to his head, but later revisions had produced better results, and the king was now hopeful of success. He was pleased with the amount of hold the goo offered, and it brought the added bonus of a pleasant pine scent that followed him wherever he went (though some of the castle staff had begun unconsciously humming Christmas carols whenever he came around).

The king checked his reflection again and addressed the men who sat around the table: "Nobles, I'm worried. The Royal Spy has sent word that Tarnation has a new Secret Weapon, but he has not yet been able to find out what it is."

"Again?" said a bored looking man in a bearskin cape.

"How's that, Duke Ellington?" said the king.

"Forgive me, your Royalness," said the duke, "but you said the same thing last time we prepared for battle—and the time before that. It seems Tarnation has a new Secret Weapon every turn of the millstone. First it was the Mirror of Pervasive Blindness, intended to reflect sunlight into our eyes and deprive our soldiers of their sight—but the day of battle was overcast. Then they had the Amulet of Irresistible Sleepiness that was supposed to put us all into a trance, but they couldn't find a soldier who could hold it aloft without slipping into a stupor and falling face-first into the mud. Then there was the Bow of Significant Distance and the Catapult of Unprecedented Range. Those people have more Secret Weapons than Queen Arabella—long may she live—has shoes."

Though the king wanted to disagree, he found himself once again overwhelmed by the duke's superior logic and skill with words. "I cannot deny the truth of what you say, Duke Ellington," said the king. "My wife does indeed have a lot of shoes."

Ellington considered explaining to the king that his point wasn't actually about shoes, but decided instead to continue what he was saying and hope Engelbert would eventually catch up.

"So, as I was saying," said the duke, "every time Tarnation comes up with something new, we produce our own Secret Weapon to counter their Secret Weapon. We had the Flaming Logs of Fate, but we occupied the low ground and had to endure their taunts and rock throwing all day as the logs turned to ash while we attempted to push them up the hill with our long pikes—"

"Oh, yes," interrupted the king. "I'm glad you reminded me. Make note that next time we should make sure the logs are in position before setting fire to them."

"Noted, Your Royalness," said the Noble who had been elected to take meeting notes, scritching enthusiastically with his quill.

"Then," continued Ellington, "there were those magic beans we got from that Jack kid—but what happened when we fed them to our horses? Colic, that's all."

A Noble with a red moustache leaned toward the man next to him and whispered, "I told you we should have fed them to the men."

"My favorite so far," said Ellington, "was at the Battle of Ficus Forge when we hired that old guy to shake a stick at their army while shouting 'um-booga-booga-booga!'"

"He was reputed to be a powerful wizard," said the king, looking a little hurt, "and he came with impeccable references."

"He might as well have been your cup bearer's cup bearer for all the good he did us," replied Ellington. "My point is Tarnation comes up with some new-sounding thing, and our spy reports it to us like it's the end of the world, and then we tremble in fear—by the way, are you sure our spy isn't actually working for them?"

"Well, I suppose it's possible," admitted the king. "He has complained that he's under-paid."

"Either way," continued Ellington, "Tarnation isn't any better at coming up with Secret Weapons than we are. I say we ignore it this time; it's nothing to worry about."

"But I'm the king," said the king, "and worrying is part of my job description[‡]. Until we learn otherwise, I'm afraid we have to assume that they may really be on to something this time. For all we know they may have come up with a

---

[‡] Constitution of the Royal Kingdom of Rondolay, Section 17, Paragraph 5.

weapon capable of wiping Rondolay off the map."

The Nobles watched their king intently, each considering the seriousness of what had been said. The air seemed to thicken with tension as each of the Nobles sat silently imagining a dozen catastrophes that might await them at the hands of the terrible Tarnationals. At length, King Engelbert turned to Ellington and broke the silence.

"Do you really think my wife has too many shoes?" he said.

After the Council of War, King Engelbert returned to the Royal Bedchambers where Queen Arabella was practicing her calligraphy.

"How did the war council go, dear?" she said absently.

"Oh, you know," Engelbert said with a sigh. "Same as always."

"That's nice, dear," she said, not looking up from the parchment she was lettering.

King Engelbert seated himself at his grooming table and began trying on eyebrows. "We're going to be crushed like a glass figurine beneath a stampede of draft horses," he said.

"Glad to hear it, dear," said the queen, distracted. She was having trouble with the flourish on one of her capital letters.

Engelbert was looking doubtfully in a mirror, with two short strips of rabbit pelt stuck above his eyes. "How do I look, my little coochie-poo?"

She looked up from her work for the first time. "What?" she said.

"My eyebrows," he said. "How do I look?"

"Like your forehead is being attacked by caterpillars."

The king's expression drooped. One of the caterpillars fell off.

"Perhaps you should stick with the eyebrow pencil, dear," she said.

"Eyebrow pencil! A king can't lead an army into battle wearing eyebrow pencil!"

She was back at her calligraphy. "You're right, of course, dear," she said. "How silly of me. Perhaps the dyed lamb's wool?"

"Wool makes me itch...."

The conversation went on this way for another half hour at least, none of which was interesting enough to write down. But while we're waiting, this might be a good time to provide...

# A Brief History of a Lengthy War

The War of Prodigious Length began when Engelbert's father, King Archibald, was out riding the boundaries of his kingdom. Riding the boundaries of one's kingdom, if you had one, was a common activity among Royals of that time because polo, charity fund raisers, and photo opportunities hadn't been invented yet. Although photo ops were still way in the future, most Royals did attract groups of people called "paparazzi."

While many today believe paparazzi came into being shortly after the invention of the modern camera, nothing could be farther from the truth. In fact, the word "paparazzi" originated in Rome during the late ninth century. It was then and there that a sausage merchant named Donatello "Papa" Rozzi noticed the large crowds that gathered whenever the Pope was expected to appear and address the masses.

Papa realized the people would be hungry standing around in the hot sun all day, and devised a large wooden tray which stood out from his waist and was supported by a leather strap around his neck. He would then walk through the crowd, carrying sausage links and a bucket of spring water on the tray, shouting things in early Italian that translate roughly to "Sausage! Get yer sausage here!" To which a hungry member of the crowd might shout (in early Italian), "Papa Rozzi!

Over here! Can you change a fifty?" So it was that over time, groups of people who lie in wait to see a celebrity came to be called "paparazzi," or, in English, "stalkers."

Although the importance of Papa Rozzi's innovation is often overlooked by historians, it made him the first person ever to sell extremely overpriced and sanitarily dubious foodstuffs at public events involving a captive audience. (It also means the world's first Candy Girl was neither a girl nor a seller of candy, but was actually a grandfatherly Roman merchant who smelled strongly of sausage.)

Eventually, Papa Rozzi made so much money from this activity that he was able to hire other people and expand into multiple locations, causing him to become an early pioneer in another sanitarily dubious activity: income tax withholding. And so it was that a humble seller of sausage became not only the forerunner of our modern paparazzi, but also the patron saint of wandering hotdog sellers and Coke hawkers in sports stadiums around the world.

But I digress.

Since all forms of photography were still centuries in the future, King Archibald's small group of paparazzi followed him around all day not taking pictures. Instead, they captured memorable kingly moments by drawing on parchment with grimy stubs of charcoal. When following the king, a scene of great importance could develop in an instant, so the paparazzi had to be ready to draw at a moment's notice. Usually, the drawings looked kind of like this:

They had to be very quick. Over time, the paparazzi became geniuses at speed drawing (you don't want to play against them in Pictionary, let me tell you). The best among them were able to capture subtlety and detail that most artists can only dream of. For example, the image above is titled "The King Prepares to Mount His Noble Steed." As you can see, the king had chosen to ride his prize-winning Arabian on this occasion instead of his favorite appaloosa. Here he is on another occasion with the appaloosa:

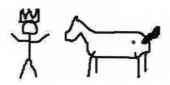

It was common for a member of the paparazzi to spend the night in a tree outside the castle wall, parchment and charcoal stub in hand, hoping to catch a glimpse through a window of something scandalous he could draw, or at least to not fall out of the tree.

Sometimes, on days when King Archibald was feeling especially peevish, he would rip the parchment from the hands of a wide-eyed paparazzi, throw it to the ground, and stomp on it, at which point the other paparazzi would snicker at their colleague's misfortune and draw as fast as their charcoal stained fingers could move.

The goal of all this activity was, predictably, money. The village tabloid, the *Royal Payne* (Heathrow Payne, proprietor), would sometimes pay as much as several pennies for a quality drawing of one of the Royals. Pictures of Royals having tantrums often fetched the highest prices. Those usually looked something like this:

(Note the artist's creative choice of portrait over landscape orientation.)

Here is another artist's work, this time in landscape:

There were no printing presses back then, so any copies of the tabloid had to be made by monks locked in dank, gloomy, stone chambers that were the early forerunners of our modern-day office cubicles. The copying took a long, long time—so long in fact that the events described in the tabloid were often more history than news by the time the copies were done. Nobody noticed, though, because no one in town could read except the Royal Family, who usually bought up all the copies to show each other their pictures in the paper and find out what their sneaky, underhanded relatives might be up to. The only times the copying delay caused problems were when the *Payne* reported rumors that one of the Royals was plotting an assassination. (In fact, there had been a duke in one of the lesser provinces who might still be alive today if the monks hadn't run short of candles in the copy room.)

All in all, it wasn't a bad way to keep up with the family. Once the pictures had been shown and the rumors dispelled, issues of the *Royal Payne* were usually preserved for posterity at one of the queen's celebrated scrapbooking parties.

Of course, the Royals loved all the attention, but they didn't want to *look* like they loved the attention. What they needed was a way to ensure they would remain in the public eye while at the same time appearing to hate being in the public eye. It was a difficult balance to maintain. This remained a problem of considerable delicacy until Shon le Peen, an inconsequential fifth cousin to the king of France, struck (quite literally) on the solution: physically attack the paparazzi. This way, any Royal, no matter how personally limited, could engage in behaviors that would have earned anyone else a drastically reduced lifespan in the local Tower of Travail, while at the same time appearing to be suffering victims of the attention they were bringing on themselves. This technique became very handy when, after the general population had learned to read, the Royals invented another profitable but subtle technique for gaining attention: the memoir. Through this device it became abundantly clear that one need not be great or heroic to be a success; one needed only to be *famous*. Soon everybody and their plow-horse were writing books about themselves, the more outrageous the better. Today our cultural luminaries still follow this time-tested path to riches, only now we call them *celebrities*.

Just in case you wanted to know all that.

\* \* \*

Anyway, the War of Prodigious Length began when King Engelbert's father, King Archibald, was out riding the boundaries of his kingdom. It was a particularly hot day—I mean a real scorcher. Archibald's horse (the appaloosa) was followed by the Royal Cupbearer on horseback, who was in turn trailed on foot by a panting and sweaty group of medieval paparazzi and Yippy, the Royal Wire-Haired Terrier. As the party crested a grassy rise, the king, upon seeing a massive tree on the next hilltop, said, "Let us away to yon hillock to seek respite beneath that enormous flora of great shadiness."

The Cupbearer, in keeping with his extensive training in the Rules of Royal Protocol, was like lightening in his response: "Huh?" he said.

The king sighed. "Let's go sit under that tree."

"Oh. Okay, Your Highness."

And so they went, leading the group of sun-baked peasants and a wire-haired terrier yipping maddeningly at their horses' heels (the dog, not the peasants).

What Archibald did not know was that the king of the adjoining land of Tarnation was at that moment climbing the opposite side of that hill with his Royal Hangers-On and Yes-Man, intending to sit in the same shade of the same tree. The two parties crested the hill at the same time, and met by the gnarled trunk of the ancient tree.

"Hail, King Archibald!" said Ficus, King of Tarnation. "You are looking sweaty this afternoon."

"He sure is," said Ficus's Yes-Man. "Sweaty as a ditch-digger in August."

Archibald shot the Yes-Man an annoyed look, and was surprised to see the Yes-Man was in fact a female lady who happened to be a woman. (Tarnation considered itself a highly progressive kingdom—a fact they invariably mentioned in their tourism brochures.) "Hail, King Ficus," said Archibald. "Are your saddle sores still plaguing you?"

Yippy began turning circles under Ficus's horse (an Andalusian), barking and nipping at its ankles.

Ficus winced visibly at the mention of his saddle sores. He would have to speak to Heathrow Payne about what sorts of stories he included in his newspaper. "No, dear cousin," said Ficus. "They haven't bothered me in a fortnight. And how is Queen Roberta? Still trying to lose all that weight?"

"When she sits around the castle...," began the Yes-Person.

"Oh no, you branch-of-the-family-tree-most-in-need-of-pruning," said Archibald. "She is svelte and comely since she began skipping afternoon tea and swimming laps in the moat every morning. And what of cousin Filigree? Is she still consumed by that dreadful acne...?"

You get the picture. The exchange went on this way for another half hour at least, punctuated with supportive comments from one side and dog yips from the other. The only thing worth mentioning that happened during this time is when they were interrupted by a sudden *yelp!* which was followed immediately by a wire-haired blur flying past Archibald's head. Ficus's horse stood innocently, pretending to be interested in a clump of dandelions, but looking rather satisfied with himself at the same time. (*Historical Note:* after that day, Yippy never barked at horses again, and he never nipped at the heels of anything larger than an adolescent hamster. In fact, he was so quiet and well behaved, the queen changed his name to Lucky—not because he was fortunate to have survived the ordeal, but because of the lucky horseshoe imprint that remained forever after on his rump.)

So as I was saying, after at least a half hour, when the customary state protocols were satisfied (and his saddle sores had become almost unbearable), Ficus changed the subject.

"I have been riding the boundaries of my kingdom—"

"A coincidence!" interrupted Archibald. "I have been doing the same, though it will undoubtedly take me much longer since my kingdom is so much larger than yours."

"Still living in that fairytale, I see," said Ficus. "Next you'll be chasing unicorns. Never-

47

theless, I've been riding my boundaries and we have decided to stop to rest under this tree."

"Sounds like a plan to me, oh Sagacious Monarch!" said the Yes-Person.

"Your decision is undoubtedly a wise one as we have decided the same," said Archibald. "I approve, and, if you can silence your infuriating Yes-Person, I grant permission for your party to rest under our tree."

"You...grant...permission?" said Ficus. "What in Tarnation are you talking about? This magnificent specimen of *humongus magnolius* is obviously rooted well inside *my* kingdom."

"No doubt about it, Unerringly Well-Informed Dictator," chimed the Y.P.

Archibald, his face reddening, turned to the Yes-Person. "Can't you do anything other than agree?!?!"

"Uh...yes?" said the Y.P.

"Please," Archibald said to Ficus while climbing down from his horse. "Let's not fight over it. The land of Tarnation is rich in petroleum products and gaseous emissions. Surely you do not need to claim this one, solitary tree, which so plainly stands in the kingdom of Rondolay."

King Ficus dismounted and approached Archibald. "It is plain to any *fool* that it resides in Tarnation."

"Absolutely correct, Your Royal Rightness," said the Y.P.

Archibald leaned into Ficus's face, teeth

clenched. *"Perhaps that is why it is plain to you."*

The Y.P. turned to Ficus. "I think he got you on that one."

The kings pulled their heavy broadswords.

The paparazzi started drawing.

Thus were the first blows struck in a war that would outlast both kings, and replace boundary riding as the Royal Pastime-of-Choice in both kingdoms for more than a generation. After a few minutes of swinging swords and ringing armor, both kings fell to the ground, completely exhausted. Thus it was that no one was injured in the First Battle of Humongus Magnolius except an irritating wire-haired terrier and a paparazzi who got hit in the eye with a windblown fleck of charcoal.

So they all returned to their homes in a huff, where both sides claimed victory in the battle (the Y.P. claiming it for Tarnation ["Oh, Victorious Sword Slinger!"], and the paparazzi claiming it for Rondolay), declared the tree an indispensable and priceless national treasure, and began preparing their armies.

Archibald launched out on a seven-castle speaking tour where he assured the people that the war—they called it "The Conflict of Minimal Duration" back then—would be quick, and Rondolay's victory decisive. "We're talking days, not weeks here," he said confidently.

As things turned out, he was spectacularly wrong.

The second morning after Nova's arrival at the farm was even foggier than the morning before, with a slight drizzle falling as Amethyst and her mother walked to the barn to care for the animals.

"Mother," said Amethyst, "do you think the rain will hurt the rhubarb?"

Amethyst's mother was surprised by the question. "Oh no, child. Plants like the rain. In fact, they need it." She pulled the heavy barn door open. "It's been such a long time since we've had any rain that you've forgotten—"

She stopped short.

Inside the barn, Massey Fergusson was in his bowing position again.

"My goodness!" said Amethyst's mother. "What's wrong with Massey Fergusson? Did his front legs collapse or will his back legs not bend?"

"He's okay, Mother," said Amethyst. "He's just bowing to make Nova feel welcome. You know as well as I that horses are herd animals, and Massey Fergusson has always been quick to respond to social cues with appropriate equine etiquette."

The old plow-horse climbed wearily to a standing position, looking slightly embarrassed (if such a thing is possible for a horse) at having been caught rump-up two mornings in a row.

"See, Mother? He's just fine."

"Well, that's a relief," said Amethyst's mother. "I was afraid there for a minute that he was broken."

Amethyst stooped down and climbed between the rails into Nova's stall. "There's my good boy," she said. "How's my Nova this morning?"

Nova watched her intently with his huge, deep eyes. Amethyst had never seen such an intelligent-looking animal. She held his head between her hands and stared at him. He looked regal and clever, like he was thinking about the kinds of things little girls dream about: love and galloping in the wind and eating lush grass in the sunshine. She suddenly thought he was going to speak, like he had a special secret he wanted to share with her and nobody else. Staring deeply into Nova's eyes, Amethyst became aware that he kept silent at that moment only because her mother was close enough to hear.

Either that, or because he was a horse and horses can't talk.

"Oh," said Amethyst tenderly, stroking the spot between his eyes with her fingertips. "You've got a bump on your head. What happened, boy? Did you bang your head on something?"

But the bump didn't look like an injury, and Nova didn't shy away from her touch as though it hurt him. And it was hard, like a bone, not puffy like it would have been if it were the result of blunt force trauma. In fact, the bump looked almost like it was supposed to be there, like something was growing—

"I'll be in the fields," said Amethyst's mother, picking up a hoe and heading out the barn door, readying herself for battle with the hardy thistle plants that grew like needley stalks of iron between the rhubarb rows.

In his stall, Nova watched Amethyst, continuing to not say anything.

"Are you hungry, boy?" she said, reaching for a basket of rhubarb stalks. "Would you like some rhubarb?"

At that, Nova bowed his head deeply then raised it again in a very definite "Yes" motion.

Amethyst stared in astonishment at what the little foal had just done. She couldn't believe he wasn't sick of the stuff by now.

"Was that a Yes, boy? Are you hungry?"

He did it again. Down, up.

She fed him a rhubarb stalk.

If Amethyst's mother hadn't already left the barn, it's debatable whether she would have found Nova's apparent understanding of the English language any more surprising than her daughter did, which was not at all. As you may have deduced from some of her previously described life choices, there were times when Amethyst's mother appeared not to be on speaking terms with reality. But she meant well, and Amethyst loved her, so we'll try not to be too hard on her, okay?

Amethyst's failure to appreciate what had just happened, on the other hand, was almost understandable. Almost. Being quite young and having limited experience with horses, she didn't initially understand that they do not as a rule understand spoken English. She assumed that Nova, being little more than a baby, was normal and that Massey Fergusson, who had always had a reputation for being tired and somewhat cantankerous, had never responded to verbal cues because he was merely grumpy. It was a notion that would have offended the old plow-horse greatly, if such a thing were possible for a horse.

Amethyst finished up with the horses, then set to milking the cow, who produced an unprecedented amount of milk, nearly covering the bottom of a small wooden bowl.

"Gracious, Petunia," said Amethyst, squeezing away. "If you keep this up, we're going to have to invest in a bucket." There was so much milk, in fact, that Amethyst decided to leave a little for Clawed, who, draped over one of the barn rafters like a dry-rotting blanket, emitted a sleepy "yeoow" as if to say, "Thanks, kid. I'll get to it later."

Amethyst put the milk bowl into her now-empty rhubarb basket and went out the door. When she turned to close the door behind her, she—

There was a man watching her from behind the corner of the barn. I say it was a man because it was, but through the fog Amethyst got only the indistinct impression of someone draped in a ratty bathrobe and suffering a rampant case of bed head.

Amethyst dropped her basket in shock. "Who's there?" she called.

At Amethyst's challenge, the figure, emitting a noise that sounded a lot like *"gaak!,"* ducked back behind the barn.

"Stop!" she called, forgetting her basket and running to where the figure had been. She rounded the corner and stopped. There was nothing there but silent, swirling fog.

"Father, if that's you, the house is over this way!"

No answer.

"Come to think of it," she muttered to herself, "the house is over this way even if that isn't you."

Amethyst turned suddenly and ran smack into another person.

"Did you call me?" the other person said.

"Oh, Mother! You startled me! I saw someone watching me from behind the barn! He disappeared into the fog when I called to him."

"Was it your father?"

"I couldn't tell. I don't think so."

"Oh. Pity," said Amethyst's mother. "Are you sure you didn't just imagine it?"

"I'm sure, Mother. Look." Amethyst pointed at the ground.

In the soft earth by the corner of the barn were the prints of two moccasined feet. There was a track of footprints leading up to the corner, and another track leading away, but right at the corner was a pair of footprints that were deeper and more pronounced than the others, footprints that looked like they had been made by a pair of feet not moving for a long time.

"How odd," said Amethyst's mother. "Well, if we are going to have strangers lurking about, I think we'd better go into the house until this fog clears."

The fog was gone by late morning, burned off by sunshine that warmed the skin and filled Amethyst's heart with the joy of being alive. She was allowed to take Nova out of the barn on a lead rope, though Mother had said she must stay in the yard between the house and barn. For more than an hour, the sounds of girly laughter and horsey whinnying filled the air as she and Nova nuzzled and chased each other in circles. It was good to hear Amethyst so happy.

It was the middle of the afternoon before Amethyst's mother realized she hadn't heard a sneeze all day.

It rained that night. It wasn't a violent or excessive storm, just a gentle but prolonged soaking that was exactly what people who know about such things would have said was perfect for rhubarb.

The next morning the sky was clear, the sun was warm, and Nova had a horn.

Amethyst and her mother stood in the barn

doorway, staring in mute astonishment.

The little white horse had a four-inch horn extending from the spot where the bump had been the day before. The horn was just over an inch wide at the base, and formed a perfectly tapered corkscrew to the tip. It looked like it had been carved from the biggest pearl in the world: shiny, translucent, and slightly iridescent, reflecting muted but beautiful rainbow colors that shifted with the light.

The moment had come at last. Standing together in wonder, it finally dawned on our heroines that Nova, the frail white foal with the impossibly intelligent eyes, was in fact—

"A rhinoceros!" exclaimed Amethyst's mother.

Amethyst nearly ruptured a vital organ trying to keep from laughing; she didn't want to appear disrespectful.

"No, Mother, not a rhinoceros, a *unicorn.* Don't you see he has *purple* eyes?"

"Oh, of course," said Amethyst's mother. "How silly of me."

And, just as you have suspected all along, Dear Reader, it was perfectly true. Nova's unicorn-ness was finally showing in a way not even Amethyst and her mother could miss.

"A unicorn!" exclaimed Amethyst. "Mother, do you know what this means?"

"I sure do, that it's a good thing we didn't eat him."

"No, Mother—uh, I mean, *yes,* but more

than that, unicorns bring blessings on their owners!"

"Why ever would we need that?" said Amethyst's mother. "We already have all the rhubarb we can eat without poisoning ourselves. What could we possibly want with more?"

# The Taxman Cometh

As everyone knows, wars are expensive propositions, and have been so ever since the invention of metal. Military conflicts were far more affordable before soldiers had to worry with broadswords and armor and helmets: sticks and rocks were in ready supply nearly everywhere, and rarely cost anything at all.

Metal was invented when an ambitious but socially sensitive caveman named Grunk had an argument with his new bride during their wedding reception. Wedding receptions were much different back then because a lot of the elements of modern wedding receptions—like crepe paper bells, obnoxious disc jockeys, and buildings—hadn't been invented yet. At Grunk and Eileen's reception, the newlyweds and their guests were seated around the celebratory bonfire as the couple received wedding gifts from the clan. The trouble began as soon as they removed the first gift from its wrapper (a banana leaf tastefully decorated with interlocking hearts).

It was a rock.

Eileen was thrilled. Grunk was not.

Now, for a caveman, getting a rock as a wedding present wasn't a problem at all; nearly all caveman presents—wedding, birthday, bar mitzvah, and otherwise—were rocks. The problem for Grunk was the *color* of the rock, for it was a rusty red that came off on his fingers, and he had decided when they announced their engagement to the clan that they would ask specifically for white rocks[§]. Eileen had said she wanted red rocks because they would match better the walls of any caves they were likely to find in the area, but Grunk had settled the matter—at least in his own mind—explaining "white new black."

When they unwrapped the second package—another red rock—Grunk's disappointment grew. There were white rocks all over the place. How hard could it be to find a white rock?

By the third red rock, Grunk was irritated.

By the forth, he was suspicious. *She did this. She blew our chance to get a matching set of white stoneware because she told everyone we wanted the red pattern.*

When the fifth and final gift turned out to be another red rock, Grunk's normally polite social sense snapped. He grabbed the rock, jumped to his feet, and pointed a finger at Eileen: "You tell clan give red rock!" he accused. This drew a series of gasps and grunts (which may or may not have been intended as actual words—Grunk could hardly ever tell for sure) from the wedding guests. Eileen looked surprised by the outburst, but said nothing. Grunk could see in

---

[§] In the ages since Grunk and Eileen's wedding, people have discovered other types of white rocks, and have given them names to tell them apart. The type of rock Grunk wanted is now called "quartz."

her eyes that it was true.

Disgusted, he flung the rock into the bonfire and stormed away (cavemen used to throw things and storm away even more often than they gave each other rocks).

After the outburst, the bride awkwardly thanked the guests for coming, then lumbered off to find Grunk. The bride's Uncle Grack (who had caught the garter), in an early forerunner of the modern *faux pas,* commented that, given the stone-throwing incident, he feared the marriage was off to a "rocky" start. The pun was met with a chorus of groans (which may or may not have been intended as actual words).

Some time later, Grunk, after making up with Eileen, decided to retrieve the fifth gift in order to have the complete set. But when he sifted through the ashes of the bonfire, he was surprised to find part of the fifth gift had melted into something that was no longer rock. It was...something else: iron.

Grunk saw at once the novelty of this new substance and immediately set out to produce more, intending to barter with his friends and become the wealthiest man in the tribe. As has been the case with many of history's pioneers, though, Grunk didn't realize the true value of what he had, and spent the remainder of his life trying to interest his neighbors in his line of iron-dribble wedding gifts.

Once people figured out how to separate

the metal part of rocks from the rock part of rocks, everything changed. After that, warfare required *preparation* (if you were entertaining any hope of winning, that is) and preparation requires labor, and, as we all know, labor requires *money*. This led to the invention of another hazard of civilization: *taxes.*

Before coins, people used stones for money. Stones were very inconvenient forms of money for two reasons: one, when you dropped the smaller ones on the ground it was often difficult to determine which rocks were the money you had just dropped and which were just rocks, and, two, it was a bummer when you had dragged a large-denomination rock all the way to the local market only to find out the guy couldn't make change for it (from whence arose our modern habit of describing something that isn't any fun as being a "drag"). Stones also had the disadvantage of being easy to counterfeit; all you needed to come up with a convincing fake was a shovel and a strong back.

This led to the invention of coins.

The invention of coins was an exceedingly convenient development for tax collectors. Prior to coins, collecting taxes was often a strenuous and dangerous job, even before taking into account that every person you contacted wanted to cause you bodily harm (Tax Collector was ranked second on Rondolay's list of *Most Hazardous Occupations in the Kingdom,* right behind Archery Range Arrow Retriever). This is because, before coins, taxes were often paid with boulders, live chickens, bulls, watermelons, and the occasional rabid boar.

Thus did the anger control issues of an illiterate caveman named Grunk inadvertently bring about both metal and taxation, polar opposites on *Ratzendinger's Continuum of Useful Historical Innovations.* You win some, you lose some, I guess.

And all that stuff I have written about above brought about what I am going to write about next, which was the arrival at Amethyst's farm, on a beautiful morning nearly a week after the appearance of Nova's horn, of the Royal Tax Collector.

Nova's horn was now ten inches in length. He stood in silent nobility, watching through the rails of his stall as Amethyst milked Petunia (who was not only giving more milk than Amethyst's mother knew what to do with, but was actually beginning to add a little padding to her normal, painfully boney figure [the cow, that is, not Amethyst's mother, though her mother could have used a few pounds as well]).

Massey Fergusson looked as though he was putting on weight as well, and the dull, spent look that had held his eye for so long seemed to be brightening. In fact, people who know about such things in horses have told me he looked exactly as if he was beginning to age backward.

The positive changes that seemed to infect

the very air around him had no effect whatsoever on Clawed. He was still the undisputed holder of the "Laziest Cat in the World" title, paws down. It was a fact that would have pleased him very much, if experiencing such emotion had not been more effort than he was willing to exert.

Amethyst's mother had just left her daughter with her hands full (literally) in the barn, and was crossing the little clearing to the house when the Royal Tax Collector rode up on horseback, followed by his hunched, eye-patched assistant driving a wagon containing a half-dozen loose-rolling watermelons and seven baskets of newly crushed chicken eggs.

"Good morning, esteemed taxpayer!" said the Royal Tax Collector, stopping his horse next to the low wall that ran between the house and barn[**].

"Hello, Robber," said Amethyst's mother, cheerfully. "Tuesday again already?"

"Afraid so."

"Seems like it was Tuesday just a week ago."

"Time flies. And please, call me 'Ro-*bear*.' It's the French pronunciation of 'Robert.'"

"Isn't that what I said?" said Amethyst's

---

[**] The wall was made of smooth stones that had been fished from the nearby riverbed. It (the wall, not the riverbed) had been built by Amethyst's grandfather before he had died, which, if you are going to build a wall, is by far the best time to do it.

mother.

"You said 'Robber.' My name is 'Ro-bear.'"

"That's what I said: Robber."

"Ro-bear!"

"I'm not hearing a difference."

"Well then would you please just call me 'Rob'?" The man on the horse was flustered. He and Amethyst's mother had this same conversation, or one very much like it, almost every Tuesday.

"Okay, *Rob*. I would offer you and your misshapen henchman a cup of water," said Amethyst's mother, "but you took the dishes on your last visit." Then, as an afterthought, she added, "Though I did find a couple of spoons you overlooked."

"Thank you for the generous thought, kind peasant"—

(Amethyst's mother considered interrupting him to correct his misidentification of her lower social class, but thought better of it.)

—"woman. It is true the trail has been long and the dust has been, uh, dusty." He scanned the place with his eyes, and his expression became one of puzzlement. "Though it seems to have rained here."

"It does that sometimes," said Amethyst's mother. "Falls right out of the sky."

"What I mean is we have ridden all over the kingdom this morning, and your farm is the *only* place it appears to have rained."

"Go figure," said Amethyst's mother.

"Yes. Quite." Robber—uh, *Ro-bear* ran his eyes over the place, looking for anything new, anything to indicate an increase in prosperity since his previous visit. "Well, what have you got to report? I see the rhubarb is flourishing. It looks as though it's doing especially well near the barn."

Amethyst's mother looked and saw with astonishment that he was right. The rhubarb was less brown than she had ever seen it, and there was a large thistle plant next to the barn that looked positively sick. For the first time in her memory, the weeds were dying and the rhubarb wasn't. Even the begonias were thriving. The sight was almost as shocking as the realization that someone had just used the word "flourishing" to describe a non-vermin life form on her farm. She was quite sure that had never, *ever* happened before.

The Tax Man interrupted her thoughts: "Taxes do take a chunk, but we must all pay our fair share, what with the war on and all."

"That crazy war," she said. "It's been going on for most of my lifetime, and I don't think the king even knows what it's about anymore."

"Ours is not to wonder why, good woman," said Ro-bear.

"I know, I know. But I'm not sure what you are going to take...unless the king wants our baby unicorn."

Ro-bear burst into laughter. "Oh, my dear, impoverished woman! You slay me. That's the spirit, though. Keep your humor to the last."

Amethyst's mother stood awkwardly; she hated it when everybody got the joke except her, especially when she was the one who had told it.

"I know times are difficult," Ro-bear said seriously. "But still, we must all do our part."

"I'll get the spoons," she said.

Ro-bear was still chuckling about the unicorn quip, smiling to himself as he watched her go into the house.

But the one-eyed wagon driver wasn't smiling. As he stared toward the slightly open barn door, his one good eye bugging out as though it were trying to compensate for the bad one, his mouth was actually hanging open a little.

## Nova is Gone!

On the morning that Nova disappeared, Amethyst awoke with a feeling that something was terribly wrong. The sky was overcast and threatening, as if all the rottenness that should have come to Amethyst and her mother had been held back for a time, and was about to dump on them all at once.

Amethyst put on her dress and hurried out of the house. The barn door was hanging partly open.

Nova was not in his stall.

Amethyst called frantically to her mother. A quick search of the farm turned up no unicorns, but did find a set of unicorn hoofprints alongside two sets of human hoofprints leading from Nova's stall to a set of wagon tracks that led out onto the main road.

It was true.

Nova was gone.

Amethyst and her mother stood speechless, facing down the lane and holding hands, eyes searching for some sign of Nova, minds trying to make some sense of what had happened.

They couldn't do it.

Amethyst, seeing no other viable options at that point, shattered the silence with a volcanic sneeze (*Aaaaaaaaaa-chooooo!!!!*)...and then began to cry.

* * *

Amethyst had never been one to meet misfortune sitting down. She did not know how much an eight-year-old girl two social classes below "peasant" could do to locate and repossess a mystical creature most people didn't even believe existed, but she knew deep in her heart she had to do *something*.

So she threw herself onto her bed and cried really hard.

After an hour of this, she became dissatisfied with the results, sat up, and wiped her eyes.

"Well, I'm not going to get Nova back that way," she said. "I must think of something more productive, something that will incentivize other people to help me."

Then it came to her.

She went for her crayons[††].

---

[††] Now, I'll bet you're thinking, "Crayons? Did they even have crayons back then?" Great question. The answer is a resounding, unequivocal "Sort of." In the Middle Ages, the word "crayons" really meant "sticks that have been burned on one end to make a charcoal tip." (These were similar to the drawing instruments used by the king's paparazzi, monks in copy chambers, and graffiti artists and vandals throughout the kingdom—it really wasn't a very colorful age, when you stop and think about it.) But their inability to make beautiful colors didn't stop the marketing departments of Middle Aged crayon manufacturers from naming the different crayons like we do today. Amethyst had several such burned sticks, which had been bundled together and given names like "Cornflower" and "Burnt Umber." In the Middle Ages, "Cornflower" and "Burnt Umber" really meant "Black." Of the 11 crayons Amethyst had (there were 12 originally, but she'd lost the "Black" one), the

Amethyst spent the next two days nailing a series of hand-made fliers in strategic places throughout town. When she had finished nailing the last one into place, she stepped back to admire her handiwork:

*Lost:* *one majical unicorn, all white with one strate horn in the middle of his forehead, likes strawberries, ansers to the name "Nova." Brings enormous luck and prospearity to anyone who poseses him. In fact, he was well on his way to making us rich when he disappierded.*

*Reward:* *a basket of pre-wilted rubarb stalks. If found, please return to the third farm on the rite on the Road of Desolation heading out of town. Thank you.*

At first the response to the fliers was underwhelming, largely because, as has been mentioned before, no one in the town could read (Amethyst herself had gone to Heathrow Payne for help with the writing part). She had, however, included on each of the fliers a drawing of a unicorn, though honestly it might easily have been mistaken for a spinning wheel or a battering ram or a water buffalo—

"Pardon me, lassie!" came a gruff voice from behind her.

---

only color name that was even remotely accurate was "Burnt Umber," and even that was only accurate in the "burnt" part.

Amethyst turned around and was surprised by a pair of emerald-colored eyes looking her right in the face. It was a dwarf. He looked to be about 60 years old, and was wearing perfectly fitting reddish-brown leather armor and a well-trimmed goatee. He spoke with a Scottish accent, which wasn't that unusual: everybody spoke with a foreign accent back then because America hadn't been invented yet.

"I see from your flier that you're looking to buy a battering ram," said the dwarf.

"Oh no, good sir," replied Amethyst. "I've lost my unicorn, and this is part of my public awareness campaign to get him back."

"Oh," said the dwarf, looking at the flier on the wall and tilting his head. "Unicorn, huh?"

"Yes, good sir. I'm afraid I've never been much of an artist."

"You can say that again. Well, in that case, would you please stop hammering things to the side of my store? It's making quite a racket in there."

"Your store?" Amethyst looked up and saw a sign hanging from a wooden post:

## Chop-n-Maul

*Gently Used Weppons For All Oakasions*

Gunter Flintlock, Proprietor

"Please forgive me!" said Amethyst. "I did

not mean to bother anyone. I've been a bit preoccupied getting my fliers up."

"I recognize you," said the dwarf. "You're that plaintive little rhubarb seller."

"That's right," said Amethyst. "My name is Amethyst. And you are...?" She looked up at the hanging sign again. "I'm sorry," she said, "I can't read."

"Neither can I," said the dwarf, "but it's a great sign, isn't it? I had Heathrow Payne help me with it."

"It shows," she said.

"I'm Gunter Flintlock, and this is my store, the *Chop-n-Maul*. Come inside. I want to talk to you."

He held the door for her and she went in.

## At the Chop-n-Maul

After a few moments, Amethyst's eyes adjusted to the dimness, and she saw a blacksmith's dream: racks of battleaxes, maces, and breastplates; display cases containing ornate daggers and oiled crossbows; polished swords mounted on the walls behind the service counter; helmets perfectly aligned along a shelf near the ceiling; full suits of armor standing at attention in the corners. There was only one customer in the place, a burly, scowling man with an intimidating capacity for hair growth. He looked up from shuffling through a bin of chainmail to regard Amethyst warily.

"What a beautiful place you have here," said Amethyst.

"Well, thank you, lass," said Gunter, climbing to a platform behind the counter. "I don't mind saying I'm quite proud of it. From personal defense all the way up to full scale invasions, the Maul satisfies all your armed combat needs. I keep the larger weapons—battering rams, catapults, that kind of stuff—out back."

"How nice!" said Amethyst politely. "Wow, those look dangerous!" She was pointing to a row of wicker baskets with daggers, knives, and tiny hand axes poking outward at odd angles.

"Ah, you've noticed my gift baskets," said Gunter with a trace of pride in his voice. "They're my own invention. Each one is a complete collection of small hand weapons. They make great gifts at the birth of male children, congratulations on battlefield promotions, that sort of thing. The trick is all in the arrangement—"

"Hey, dwarf!" growled the hairy customer. He was standing at a display stand of gauntlets[‡‡]. "How much for these gloves?"

"Gunter."

"What?"

"My name is Gunter. I prefer not being called 'dwarf,' if you don't mind. And the gauntlets are six silver pieces."

"Six!" retorted the man. "I wouldn't give you half that! Did you have a career in highway robbery before you opened this store?"

"Actually, yes, but that's another story," said Gunter. "The gauntlets are on special this week: two gloves for the price of one pair."

"Oh, you're a funny one, you are," growled Hairy. Then he added with an extra scowl, "Dwarf!"

Gunter held the customer's gaze for a moment longer before turning back to Amethyst.

"So, lassie," he said, "tell me about your unicorn."

---

[‡‡] A "gauntlet" is a metal glove, like you would see a knight in shining armor wearing. It is ideal for protecting the hands while sword fighting, feeding a chisel-fanged deathsnipe, or unclogging an electric garbage disposal. The less popular version was the "metal mitten," which is ideal for nothing.

She did, beginning at the beginning. As she talked, Gunter appeared to listen attentively, but Amethyst had the vague impression that one of his eyes followed the hairy customer as he moved about the store. Amethyst had just reached the part about Nova's disappearance when the customer interrupted.

"Okay," said Hairy. "Well, nothing worth buying in this store." He turned a little too quickly and reached for the door.

In a blur of color—mostly reddish brown—and a flash of steel, Gunter vaulted over the counter. There was a flurry of motion too quick for Amethyst to comprehend, and the customer was suddenly on the floor looking up at Gunter, who was holding a dagger to the man's throat.

"I believe you forgot to pay for these," said Gunter, pulling a pair of gauntlets from under the man's tunic.

"I w-was only j-jesting, n-noble merchant!" cried the man on the floor. "Here, the m-money is in my coin bag!"

Gunter let the man up off the floor, but kept the dagger ready.

The hairy growler was still hairy, but no longer growling. In fact, he now seemed more like a frightened puppy. His hands shook as he fumbled to retrieve some coins from his bag. "Here, take some extra—for your trouble!"

"Well, thank you," said Gunter, taking the coins and handing over the gauntlets. "Pleasure doing business with you." He returned his dagger to its sheath.

"Yeah. Same here." Hairy went to leave, but stopped midway out the door and turned back to Gunter. "Hey, dw—uh, esteemed shop-keeper, I'm putting together a band of adventurers to explore a distant dungeon that is rumored to contain a sulfur dragon. Would you consider joining us? We could use a good, uh, less-tall-than-average person in our company."

"I'm flattered by your offer, laddie," said Gunter. "I'd have jumped at such a chance in my younger days, but I'm afraid I've become too frail and slow in my old age."

"Right," said Hairy, looking like he might not entirely agree with Gunter's assessment of himself. Amethyst thought for a moment that Hairy was going to say something more, but he just shook his head and left.

"So, Amethyst," said Gunter. "You were telling me how you misplaced your unicorn."

"I didn't misplace him, sir. He was stolen from me."

"Stolen? You sure he didn't just run away?"

"Quite sure, sir. The tracks left behind indi-cate he was loaded onto a wagon and taken in the night."

"Sounds like you're going to need help," said Gunter.

"I cannot do everything, but I can do something. I'm hoping to rally the unicorn-loving public with strategically placed fliers."

"Hmmm....." Gunter stroked his goatee

thoughtfully. "That reminds me of a story I heard once a long time ago, a legend about a man of great mystery and power, with an unnatural fondness for horses. He may be able to help you."

"Who is he?" said Amethyst.

"No one knows his real name, or even if he ever had one. He is known now only as..."— Gunter looked right and left to be sure no one could overhear—"...the *Hoarse Whisperer.*"

"Whooooooooooooa," said Amethyst under her breath. "How can he help?"

"It is rumored he is part of a Dark and Far-Reaching Network of Intrigue, and that he can even talk to animals."

"I talk to animals," said Amethyst. "I used to talk to Nova all the time."

"Ah," said Gunter, leaning in for dramatic effect. "But did they ever talk back?"

Amethyst had to think about that one. "Not that I ever noticed," she said.

"Perhaps he can have his network of animal spies search for your unicorn," said Gunter.

"How do I find him?" said Amethyst.

"That's the hard part. No one has ever seen him. I've heard he lives alone, in a crack in the rocks somewhere near Anxiety Mountain, in the Foothills of Disquiet. But I have a contact who may know how to find him. I will check tonight. Come back tomorrow to see if I have been successful."

## The Quest Begins

The next morning Amethyst rose with the sun and hurried to tend the animals. It seemed to her that Petunia produced less milk than in recent days. If the decrease continued they would soon be back to measuring her output by the thimble-ful.

Amethyst took the milk into the house then headed out the front door. "I'll see you later, Mother," she called back over her shoulder. "I'm going to the Maul!"

"Have a good time, dear," said her mother. "Be sure to stay out of trouble, and be back in time for supper."

Amethyst flashed a winning smile. "If we're having any!" she said. And then she was gone.

The walk to town seemed to pass quickly. Amethyst's spirits were lifted by Mr. Flintlock's offer to help, and by the time she reached the Chop-n-Maul she was more hopeful than at any time since Nova had disappeared. As she approached, Gunter was already outside waiting for her.

"Good morning, Mr. Flintlock," she said. "Was your contact able to help? Did you find out where..."—she looked left and then right—"...*he* lives?"

"I did," said Gunter. "It is quite a walk, but we should be able to make it in a couple of hours."

"We? You're coming with me?" said Amethyst.

"What, I'm going to send an eight-year-old girl on a quest like this all by herself?" said Gunter. "Besides, I've always wanted to see a unicorn."

"Oh, thank you, noble sir!" cried Amethyst. "Truly you are larger than your external stature would suggest."

"You are kind to notice," said Gunter. "Now, let's get you outfitted for an adventure. I have some leather armor left over from the Great Gnome Uprising that should fit perfectly over that dustrag of a dress you're wearing. It comes with a matching dagger and sheath."

"But sir," said Amethyst, "I have no money to pay for these things."

"That's okay," said Gunter. "Just give me some rhubarb later. You can pretend it's valuable, and I'll pretend I want it. Besides, I'll never sell the armor. Demand for gnome-sized leather mail dried up after the gnomes lost the uprising."

"Again, thank you, kind sir."

They turned to go into the Maul.

"Mr. Flintlock?"

"Yes, lass?" said Gunter.

"That contact you used for locating the Hoarse Whisperer—is it some kind of secret military contact?"

"Nah," said Gunter. "My mother is friends with the woman who does his laundry. Now let's

78

get you ready."

Thirty minutes later, they started on the road out of town. Amethyst was encased in a suit of polished leather just like Gunter's. Walking side by side, they could have been mistaken for twins, except that she was taller, younger, and a spindly little girl without a goatee. She carried crusts of bread that Gunter had wrapped in a napkin. Gunter had a military surplus water bottle tied to his belt, and he carried a battleaxe which he used much like a walking stick when he wasn't using it to slice the heads off of roadside dandelions.

For the first part of the journey Amethyst chattered non-stop about Nova and the Hoarse Whisperer and the Foothills of Disquiet. Would the Hoarse Whisperer be willing to help them? Would his animal friends be able to find Nova? Would the little unicorn even remember her? These things, and many others, churned anxiously in the eight-year-old's mind until they found the escape hatch of her mouth. While Amethyst jabbered on, Gunter walked in silence, pretending to listen to some of what she said and actually listening to the rest. At length, Amethyst reached the end of her worries and threw the conversation into a turn.

"So tell me about yourself," she said. "How did you come to own the Maul?"

"Well," Gunter said, "that's kind of a long story."

"It's kind of a long walk," replied Amethyst. "Where are you from originally?"

"I was born in Scotland, in a village on the banks of Loch Dedoor."

"Were your parents also...uh—"

"Dwarves?" said Gunter.

"Arms dealers," said Amethyst.

"I suppose, in a manner of speaking," said Gunter. "Old Dad was officially a blacksmith—at least I think that's what it said on his sign—but he made the best broadswords for miles around."

"Why did you leave?"

"Well," said Gunter, considering the best way to say it. "I sort of had to. I'm afraid I was something of a juvenile delinquent. You see, everybody else in my family was normal size—except my little brother, Hunter. He was actually a giant. So when it came to activities with my friends, it was always 'Hunter, come play on our ball team! Hunter, come sheep-tipping with us! Hunter, come torment the sea monster in the loch with us!' And with me it was, 'Gunter, we've lost the ball down the sewer again. Could you wiggle down there and get it for us? Gunter, we need some bait to lure the monster ashore; how fast can you swim?'"

"That's horrible!" said Amethyst, aghast. "You boys should have known better than to torment a harmless sea monster!"

"Well," continued Gunter, "after a while I became angrier and angrier. It was bad enough being the least tall person in the village, but when your little brother is actually four feet taller than you—well, I think you can see how it could wear on one's sense of self worth."

"That must have been terrible for you!" said Amethyst. "What did you do?"

"Well, I started running with some bad people and did some things I'm not proud of. That's when the local constable and I decided it would be better for all involved if I left Loch Dedoor before he locked 'dedoor' of my cell.

"After that I drifted from place to place for a while. After a few years, I fell in with this band of dwarves who had a fondness for jewels."

"You were a jewel thief?" asked Amethyst.

"Not stealing," said Gunter. "Mining. We spent our days underground digging priceless gems out of the hard earth. Sometimes, during economic downturns, I find myself wishing I could remember where that mine was.

"Anyway, one day we met this young girl who was lost in the woods. A beauty, she was, young and as innocent as a newborn. I was against the idea, but the others voted to let her stay with us. It wasn't easy at first, and I was pretty upset about the whole situation. I mean, there we were, seven bachelors jammed into this tiny cottage, far more concerned with acquiring jewels and treasure than personal hygiene, and along comes this beautiful, dainty creature and plops right down in the middle of us. I was a mean, angry cuss back then. I tried being mean to her, but she'd only tease me and call me 'Grumpy.' After a while she won me over." A misty look filled his eyes and for a moment he seemed far away. "She won us all over.

"Eventually I realized this poor girl had everything going against her—no home, no family, a wicked queen trying to kill her. But even though she had nothing, she never let it get her down, you know? She was always the picture of grace and goodness. So I figured if that lass could stay upbeat in the face of all that, maybe I could, too. Maybe life wasn't so bad, after all. I mean, I had enough to eat. I had a roof over my head. And hardly anybody was trying to kill me."

"What happened then?"

"Well, she eventually married this foreign prince—named Charming, he was—and moved away. She didn't forget us completely—we got a card every Christmas and an occasional picture some paparazzi had done of her kids—but we missed her a lot. The boys and I tried to go back to our old ways, but it just wasn't the same. We had changed."

"What did you do?"

"We split up the treasure and disbanded, went our separate ways. I've lost touch with most of them. Last I heard, Sleepy had married some woman named Drowsy or Lethargic or something and bought a bed and breakfast over in Tarnation. Dopey started a school, but he had some trouble finding parents who would pay to send their children to a place called *The Dopey Academy of Learnin' and Refinement.* The fact that he couldn't talk didn't really help, either. Bashful took some assertiveness classes and became a bigwig in the Charming administration. And I moved here and bought the Maul."

Some time later, Amethyst and Gunter had reached their destination. They stood without speaking in front of a cave entrance formed by three massive, grey boulders[§§]. The wide, high mouth of the cave was completely filled with an impossibly complex framework of rough timbers, large gears, pulleys, and pendulums, all notched together to form an intricate clockwork of death. Mounted on each pendulum, gear, and axel were gleaming blades of precisely sharpened steel. The entire contraption appeared ready to spring into motion at the slightest disturbance, instantly slashing any intruders to ribbons. A narrow, twisting walkway of boards was suspended above the ground by ropes. Amethyst could barely make out a wooden door with a welcome mat set into the wall at the far side of the contraption.

A sign posted outside the cave read:

*To make it through the Cogs of Doom*
*And enter in my cave*
*Ye must confront the slashing terrors*
*And risk a lethal shave!*

---

[§§] In the ages since our heroes stood at the entrance to that cave, people have discovered other types of grey rocks, and have given them names to tell them apart. The type of rock Amethyst and Gunter were looking at is now called "granite."

84

*The Cogs are wound and wait to spring*
*If entrance is yer notion*
*A step inside will trip the trap*
*And set the Cogs in motion*

*So duck and dive with nimbleness*
*Or steel will cut and quarter*
*And find yer way to my front door—*
*Or find yerself much shorter!*

Below this someone had scrawled, "Or you could just go away!" and the initials "H.W."

Gunter, being a man of good humor and possessing a solid self-concept, took no offense whatsoever at the quip about finding oneself much shorter, mostly because he couldn't read. Instead, he was filled with admiration for the inventor of the automated clockwork he saw before him (but then again, he'd always had a fondness for lethal machinery).

"Diabolical genius," he said in awe. "I wonder if I could get one of these to sell back at the Maul? Maybe I could even become a regional distributor...."

"Let's go ask," said Amethyst with her usual cheerfulness.

She started toward the cave entrance.

The Lair of the Hoarse Whisperer was a dark but comfortably-appointed cavern, large enough to suit the needs of an ancient hermit while not appearing snobby. The chamber was lit by a dozen greasy candles that threw a crowd of flickering shadows onto the rocky walls. To one side, a hooded figure stooped over a fireplace, crumbling some herbs into a small cauldron of stew that he stirred with an old riding crop[***]. The figure wore a burlap robe that had once been white, but had in the years since settled into an agreeable shade of dinginess. The robe covered the figure from head to toe, making him look from a distance like a monk of the High Church—or a Jedi Knight who had used too much bleach—

*"Aaaaaaaaaaaaa-chooooo!!!!"* A sneeze from behind him shattered the silence.

The robed figure whipped around, obviously startled, raising the riding crop as if to deflect an imminent attack. "Who goes there?!" a voice demanded—croaked, really—from the darkness inside the hood.

Before him stood a young girl and an old dwarf, both impressively upholstered in leather armor. The dwarf, who was holding a beautifully

---

[***] A riding crop is a short stick used by horseback riders throughout the ages to communicate their wishes to their horses. The rider relays messages such as "speed up," "jump," "gallop," and "stop trying to scrape me off of your back by crashing me against a tree" by whapping the backside of the horse with the crop. A clever horse will sense the whapping and think, "This guy is hitting me with a stick; maybe I can scrape him off against that tree over there." Less clever horses will think they are being stung by an angry hornet, which, depending on how much practice the horse has had with bucking, can end the ride even sooner.

reconditioned battleaxe, wordlessly pulled a handkerchief from a pocket and wiped a large glop of stew from his cheek.

"Well," said the Hoarse Whisperer, "what do we have here?" He lowered the riding crop.

For the remainder of the story the Hoarse Whisperer lived up to his name. His voice came out as a strangled, scratchy, scraping sound. It was as if ultra-coarse sandpaper had learned to talk, like grooming a chalkboard with a wire dog brush, like the death shriek of a self-destructing garbage disposal, like—well, you get the idea.

The sound made Amethyst wince. "Ooooo," she said, "doesn't that hurt?" The figure seemed oddly familiar to Amethyst, as if she had seen him in a dream. It was as though—

"Doesn't what hurt?" croaked the robed figure.

"Talking like that," said Amethyst.

"Why?" challenged the voice from inside the hood. "What about the way I talk? Are you saying something is wrong with my voice? It's a fine thing to come into a man's home and insult him with the first words out of your mouth!"

Amethyst stopped short, speechless. Could it be he didn't know what he sounded like? She looked at Gunter, hoping for a verbal rescue. He just muttered a single word under his breath: "Awkwarrrrrrrrd."

The hooded figure stood motionless before them, waiting...then burst into a roar of uncontrolled laughter. "Oh, you should see the looks on your faces!" The wild laughter continued, then actually grew wilder.

Amethyst and Gunter stared.

"I'm sorry," croaked the hood. "I just love doing that to people. I figure if I'm stuck with a voice like a rusty gate hinge I might as well get some fun out of it. I tell you," he cackled, "it never gets old."

"Are you the Hoarse Whisperer?" asked Amethyst.

"With a voice like this?" croaked the hood. "Who else could I be?"

"We need your help," said Amethyst.

"I will grant any wish," said the Hoarse Whisperer. "You have proven yourselves to be of the highest caliber to have survived the slashing terrors of the Cogs of Doom!"

"Wellllllllll...," Amethyst said, exchanging a sheepish glance with Gunter, "...not so much."

"What dost thou mean, child?" said the Hoarse Whisperer.

"No slashing terrors," said Amethyst. "We went around. We came in that door over there." She pointed to a dark wooden panel set into a side wall. A sign was nailed to it stating: "Ye Olde Member's Entrance.'"

The robed figure's shoulders drooped. "Oh," he said.

"We didn't mean to break the rules or anything," explained Amethyst. "And though it's clear your Cog's are among the finest automatic security systems available for a ground-based dwelling, we just...well, we were in a hurry."

"And we didn't want to get hacked to pieces," added Gunter, stuffing the handkerchief into a pocket in his armor.

"Well, yes," agreed Amethyst. "That, too."

"I see...," said the H.W. "I must inform you that door is for family and friends *only*. Strangers, door-to-door peddlers, the occasional neighbor hermit needing to borrow a cup of lard—the slashing terrors are intended to discourage people like that from disturbing me. It works, too; the slashing terrors have cut way back on the number of visitors—get it? *Cut* back on the visitors?"

Gunter stared at the robed figure. "Yeah," he said blankly. "That's hilarious."

"Oh, never mind," continued the H.W. "Circumstances eventually forced me to have that door installed. I mean, I enjoy my privacy as much as the next hermit, but it just got to be too much having to face the Cogs of Doom every time I wanted to leave the cave to get a pack of gum or the morning edition of the *Royal Payne*, and then again on the way back. On top of that, we lost two regular members when I called an emergency meeting of the League two years ago and forgot to put the chocks in to stop the gears. So I had the door installed, though I can't say I care much for non-members using it.... I don't suppose ye'd be willing to go back out and have a go at the Cogs?"

Gunter shook his head.

"We'd rather not," said Amethyst, "if it's all the same to you. Like I said, we're in a hurry."

"And we don't want to get hacked to pieces," said Gunter.

"Oh, okay," said the H. W. "I guess there's nothing for it now that you're here. To tell you the truth," he continued, "I've been sort of expecting you." He reached up and tossed back his hood, revealing the leathered face of a very old man, topped by the wild hair of a rampant case of bed head.

"You!" Amethyst gasped. "You're the man from the fog, the one I saw sneaking around my farm!"

The H.W. nodded slightly. "Guilty as charged, little lady. I suspected you'd show up here before long, especially if the little unicorn had already begun bonding."

"How do you know about Nova?" Amethyst's eyes narrowed to suspicious slits. "What have you done with him?"

"Who, me? I didn't take him, young one, but I know who did. Let me put a pot of tea on the fire and we'll sit down and have a talk."

"There," said the Hoarse Whisperer some minutes later, pouring tea into some wooden cup-bowl things at a table where Amethyst and Gunter were seated. "Sorry I'm out of my usual peppermint tea. It's good for the voice, you know." He gingerly lowered himself onto a loose-jointed bench where he tottered briefly before settling. Amethyst had been afraid for a moment that he was going to tip headlong onto the floor; he wasn't the most stable fellow even when standing still.

"Nice place you have here," said Gunter.

"Thanks," said the H.W. "It's roomy enough for my needs, but small enough to avoid the appearance of conspicuous self-indulgence."

Gunter looked around approvingly. "I see what you mean—"

"Where's my unicorn?" interrupted Amethyst.

"Ah yes, the unicorn," said the H.W., pulling his seat closer to the table and tottering again. "Your unicorn was stolen by a band of thieves who live in Nightmare Forest. I saw them break into your barn and lead the little fellow away with a bag over his head. There were three of them, so I did not engage them in battle, but I was able to track them to their camp in the forest."

"Did they hurt him?" Amethyst watched

91

the man intently as she sipped her tea—and grimaced. It tasted like boiled grass clippings.

"No, nor will they, I think," said the H.W.

"What will they do to him?" asked Amethyst.

"I'm not sure, but a unicorn could be worth a lot of money to the right people. I suspect they plan to sell him."

"What were you doing at my farm?"

"Let me give you some expository background information," said the Hoarse. He leaned in toward the center of the table, teetering on the stool. "As you no-doubt know, I am called the Hoarse Whisperer. You may call me 'Hoarse' for short—everyone in the League does—"

"The League?" said Gunter.

"The Mystical Beast Protection League," explained the Hoarse, then added with obvious pleasure: "I've been president of the local chapter three years running."

"Is that a Dark and Far-Reaching Network of Intrigue?" asked Amethyst excitedly.

"More of an informal fraternal organization," said Hoarse. "We have membership meetings once a month; I host March and September here in the cave."

"I've never heard of the Mystical Beast Protection League," said Gunter.

"I'm not surprised," said Hoarse, deflating a little. "We're not the most popular of groups—it can be rather a long haul waiting for a minotaur or a pegasus to show up. Most people stop coming to the meetings years before they are assigned a beast to assist. We are often mistaken for one of the secret societies. If it weren't for the annual membership drives, I suspect we'd have died out long ago."

"What does the League do?" asked Amethyst.

"We care for some of the more extraordinary creatures on Earth," explained Hoarse, "some that might be misunderstood by the world in general, or exploited for their specialness."

"Is that why you were at our farm?" asked Amethyst. "Because you wanted to help Nova?"

"Exactly," said Hoarse. "League members are assigned different mystical beasts so each member doesn't need to become an expert on all the creatures we serve. It's more efficient that way. For example, Penelope Stonebank works SPF—"

"SPF? Sun Protection Factor?" asked Amethyst.

"Sprites, Pixies, and Fairies," said Hoarse, "though she handles brownies and the odd leprechaun as well. We have a fellow named Dinks who handles Ambulatory Primitives. He's in charge of Bigfoot and the Abominable Snowman—he's always having to travel up north to check on her—did you know the Abominable Snowman is really a female?"

"You don't say," said Gunter. "Well, isn't that a gullybumper."

"It's a fact," returned Hoarse. "And then

Billie and Willie Smithson, they're assigned to this sea monster that lives in some lake in Scotland—though they've never actually caught sight of it. Personally, I think it died a long time ago."

"Trust me, it's there," said Gunter. "But you've got to know where to look. You'll never find it if you listen to those people at the Loch Ness Tourism Bureau."

"Really?" said Hoarse. "I'll have to tell the Smithsons. The waterborne beasts are especially challenging because they're so hard to locate. I mean, you can spend your entire career on the lookout for your beast and never catch sight of it once.

"As for myself, I'm assigned to E.W.A.E. O.U.A.P."

"A-E-I-O-*what?*" said Gunter, his eyebrows climbing halfway up his forehead.

"Equines, with an Emphasis on Unicorns and Pegasi," said the H.W.

"And centaurs?" asked Amethyst. "I just love centaurs."

"No, centaurs are in the Hybrid class," said the H.W. "Handling them requires special training."

"Why is that?" asked Gunter.

"Well, it's probably obvious that finding you have a horse's back end every time you turn around can bring with it a whole spectrum of psychological difficulties."

"Can't say I ever thought about it before,"

said Gunter.

"Well it does," said Hoarse, "especially if the horse part is a thoroughbred—they're so highly strung. There are all kinds of problems that arise from being half-human and half-animal. For example, can you imagine the guilt that comes from being a half-animal carnivore?"

"Sounds awful," said Gunter.

"Debilitating!" exclaimed the H.W. "I can tell you with certainty there are few creatures in this world so conflicted as a beef-eating minotaur or a seafood-loving mermaid. The Hybrid Protectors are trained to help with things like that."

"I thought centaurs were only in ancient Greece," said Gunter.

"We have several chapters in Greece," said the H.W. "In fact, that's where the M. B. P. L. began. It started as an effort by a few of the philosophy types to draw attention to the ill-treatment suffered by several of the more unusual creatures of the day. There were gobs of mystical beasts back then: minotaurs, centaurs, satyrs—you name it. The League assigned at least one member to protect and assist each mystical beast, aid in physical defense, help with public image campaigns—that sort of thing. We even tried to help Medusa for a while—although there was considerable controversy over whether she qualified as a mystical beast since the only part of her that wasn't human was her hair. In the end it didn't really matter since none of the members assigned to her ever returned from the initial 'get acquainted' meeting, anyway."

"That's all fine and good," Amethyst interrupted, "and I'm sure this Medusa person and her hair were very gratified by the efforts to help them, but please may we return to the subject at hand? What are we going to do about my unicorn?"

"Well," said the H.W. "I'll do what I can, but I'm an old man."

"You can say that again," said Gunter.

The Hoarse shot Gunter an annoyed look. "So, as I was saying, I think the first thing we should do is go and find some help."

"Now you're talking," said Amethyst. "What kind of help?"

"Well, we'll need some money for what I have in mind," said the Hoarse. "Fortunately, I still have a few gold pieces the king gave me for waving my riding crop and shouting 'um-booga-booga-booga' at the army of Tarnation."

Several of the townspeople stopped what they were doing to watch as the girl, dwarf, and robed ancient passed by, moving slowly up the dusty street toward the center of town. They stopped in front of a well-kept mud and beam structure with a sign proclaiming:

*Ye Royal Rent-a-Rogue*
*Superlative Hero Representation*
*Since the Dark Ages*

Gunter held the door open as Amethyst and Hoarse entered the building.

The interior was brightly lit by medieval standards, which is to say the candles standing about the place produced enough light to tell the difference between a person and a wooden post, provided the person moved every now and then. A roundish, gruff-looking man stood behind a counter near the far wall. He slipped the quill he had been using into a small bottle of ink as Hoarse shuffled up to him.

"Good day," said the H.W. "We'd like to rent a hero, please."

The rental agent managed to keep the shock of hearing Hoarse's voice from showing on his face, but his mind was suddenly filled with an image of a battered violin being scraped by a bow encrusted with ground glass.

"Well, you came to the right place," said the rental agent. He pulled a fresh sheet of parchment from behind the counter and took quill in hand. "Short-term or long-term?"

"A single engagement, please," said Hoarse.

"Just one excursion?" The rental agent looked surprised. "Our three-quest packages are half off this week."

"Just the one, please," said Hoarse. "We need to rescue this little girl's uni—er, *pet horse.*"

The Rent-a-Rogue man looked at Amethyst in sudden recognition. "Hey, you're that girl who was hanging all those signs around town. Any luck selling your spinning wheel?"

"Oh, I wasn't selling a spinning wheel," Amethyst said cheerfully. "I was trying to find my—"

"Horse!" interrupted Gunter.

"Yes?" said Hoarse.

"Her *horse,*" Gunter said again. "Her *horse* that was taken by a band of thieves."

"Oh yes," said Hoarse. "Her horse that was taken by a band of thieves."

"The blackhearts," said the man behind the desk as he began scritching the quill against the parchment. "Sounds like a standard property recovery quest. How many thieves are we expecting to encounter?"

"Three," answered Hoarse. "They're headquartered in Nightmare Forest."

"Any of them particularly large or menacing looking?" said the agent. "There's a surcharge for extremely large opponents."

"No, not too large," said Hoarse, "but one was a woman. Is there a discount for women?"

"Sorry, no," said the agent. "You'd understand if you'd seen some of the women we've gone up against." He produced a stack of what could have been small kitchen cutting boards and set them on the counter. "So, we're looking at a single-engagement property recovery against three thieves in Nightmare Forest." He lifted the first board, which was painted with the image of a red-haired madman swinging a battleaxe. "This is Barthus the Berserker. He is one of our highest rated Certified Heroes. He's led quite a few successful adventures and quests, with a return-alive rate of 67 percent. He costs 100 gold pieces."

Gunter leaned toward Amethyst and whispered, "I know him. He's good."

"Have you got anything cheaper?" said Hoarse, looking suddenly uncomfortable at the mention of the 100 gold pieces.

"Certified Heroes begin at 100 and go up from there," said the agent. "Below that we've got the Command and Control category. They're mostly non-combatants—consultants, retired heroes, that sort of thing. They offer advice in the field, strategic planning, and sometimes conduct weekend adventure leadership workshops."

"I don't think we'd be interested in that,"

said the H. W. "What have you got for 13?"

"Thirteen?" The agent looked at Gunter. "Is he serious?"

Gunter checked his pockets and sheepishly replied, "I'm afraid so. I seem to have left my money in my other armor."

The agent looked pained. "Thirteen lands you at the bottom of the lowest category, General Mayhem. These guys tend not to live very long. In fact, I've got only one left." He walked to a side door, opened it, and bellowed, "Timmy! Get in here!"

After a moment a young man of about 18 years emerged from the doorway, wearing an apron and holding a broom.

"What's he going to do," said Gunter, "sweep them to death?" He couldn't decide which was thinner, Timmy or the broom handle.

The agent ignored Gunter's comment. "This is Timmy the Tremulous," he said. "He's new; we don't even have a brochure made up for him yet. Timmy, say hello to these fine people."

"Hello, fine people," said Timmy in a squeaky voice. He gripped the broom handle as he bowed deeply. Amethyst thought his hands appeared to be shaking.

"These folks are mounting a quest to recover this little girl's pony," said the agent. "It's in Nightmare Forest. You want it?"

"It's outside?" Timmy looked stricken. "I-I'm sorry. You know I-I just can't do outside work."

"Never hurts to ask," said the agent. He turned to the H.W. "The boy's got a touch of agoraphobia, I'm afraid."

Amethyst covered her mouth, eyes widening in alarm: "Is it catching?"

"No, young lady," said the agent. "It's not contagious. Agoraphobia means he's afraid of open spaces."

"Terrified, actually," said Timmy, his thin voice cracking like a boy entering his teen years. "My knees go all wobbly and my hands begin sweating. It's terrible."

"That's why Timmy's been marked down. He's the cheapest thing we've got, but unless he's willing to go outside, it doesn't look like he's going to be of much use to you."

"I'd love to help the young damsel," said Timmy, "but I just can't do wide open spaces."

"For pity's sake, lad," said Gunter, "it's a *forest.* Forests are hardly wide open spaces."

Timmy thought for a moment, then shook his head doubtfully. "Sorry," he said.

Amethyst saw her chances of rescuing Nova dissolving before her eyes unless she did something quickly. "Look," she said, "I understand that you're afraid, but you and I both know there's nothing out there that's any more dangerous than being inside, right?"

"You mean besides thieves and marauders and dragons swooping down from the sky and carrying me off to feed me to their young?"

"Well, yeah," she said. "Besides those. And

there are no such things as dragons."

At that, the H.W. cleared his throat as if to say something, but then thought better of it, picked up the brochure for Barthus the Berserker, and pretended to study it intently.

"Birds of prey, then," said Timmy. "Birds of prey could swoop down from the sky and carry me off to feed me to their young."

Amethyst almost had to give him that one. Considering the lack of meat on his bones—he couldn't weigh more than 90 pounds with long toenails and navel lint—it did appear his chances of being carried off by a bird of prey might be a good deal higher than average.

"Come on," she goaded. "What are you *really* afraid of?"

"You mean other than bloodthirsty mobs and being hit by boulders from space and rotten tree limbs falling on me and crushing me to death?"

"Yes, besides those, too. And a boulder from space isn't going to be stopped by a thatched roof, anyway, so you might as well be outside."

This gave him some pause. "I never thought of that," he said. "Maybe I should seek employment in a more sturdy structure. I wonder if the castle is hiring dishwashers?"

Amethyst rolled her eyes. "Besides that, you're ignoring all the hazards of life indoors, like the roof caving in and eye strain from the bad light and...and..."—she spied the fireplace in the side wall—"second-hand smoke! Why, I wouldn't

102

be surprised if ninety percent of all bodily injures occur at home."

"You're right," he said.

Amethyst was caught off guard at his admission. "I am?"

"Yes. I have never given second-hand smoke the dread it probably deserves."

"You're heavily invested in excuses, aren't you?" Amethyst continued. "Face it. What you're really afraid of is people. You're afraid they'll hurt you, that they'll expose your best-hidden weaknesses, find you inadequate, and laugh at you. Deep down, you're really afraid of being embarrassed, aren't you?"

"No," he said. "That's a new one, though now that I think about it I'm amazed it never occurred to me to be afraid of that before. I'm going to add it to my list."

"But you don't have to!" erupted Amethyst. "You're a Hero!"

"No, 'Hero' is two categories above me."

"You know what I mean!" exclaimed Amethyst. "You fight for the weak! You defend the innocent! Stand up for yourself! I believe in you, Timmy the Tremulous! I believe that on some level, deep down, you know you are equal to this challenge. Remember, danger is sometimes real, but fear is always a choice!"

He appeared to consider this. He was impressed by this little girl's spunk, and some of what she said made sense to him.

But, no, it was no use.

"In that case," he said. "I'm afraid I'll have to choose fear. I'm sorry. I just can't."

Although Amethyst, Gunter, and Hoarse were forced to set out for Nightmare Forest without their hired hero, the sun was shining, the air was pleasant, and their moods soon bounced back from the Rent-a-Rogue boondoggle. They were an odd sight traveling down the road: a fit and focused dwarf having to stop occasionally to wait for an eight-year-old girl who had to stop occasionally to wait for a stooped old man in a burlap robe. Though they hadn't known each other long, they found themselves becoming friends as they walked, united by their common desire to help a largely imaginary creature defeat impossible odds in a partly made-up story.

The H.W., looking to pass the time, decided this was an ideal opportunity to reveal his previously hidden—*well* hidden—talent for telling horse jokes. Amethyst and Gunter came quickly to wish it had remained hidden.

"What do you know if you find a horse-shoe?" said the H.W.

"I don't know," said Gunter. "What?"

"That somewhere in the kingdom there's a horse running around in his socks." The H.W. burst out laughing. "Oh, I've got a ton of 'em."

"Careful," said Gunter, splitting a roadside thistle plant with a swoop of his battleaxe. "Don't forget I'm armed."

"Fine," said the H.W., "so you don't like

jokes. What would *you* like to talk about?"

"Penguins," said Gunter.

"Penguins?" said the H.W.

"Aye. I love the little beggars. In your travels with the MBPL, have you ever run across any penguins?"

"You believe in penguins?" the H.W. said, incredulous. "Some folks will fall for anything."

At that point Amethyst, sensing the warm feeling of friendship was being threatened after only a few paragraphs, jumped in with stories of Nova, rhubarb, and her life on Earth so far. These she punctuated occasionally with strategically placed sneezes.

The sun was low in the sky when our heroes arrived at the edge of Nightmare Forest. They stopped there to share the bread and water Gunter had brought.

"I feel sick," said Amethyst, looking even worse than she sounded.

"Nova is feeling it, too," said the H.W., "maybe even worse than you are."

"Why is that?" asked Amethyst.

"You said Nova had grown a horn," said the H.W. "That only happens when a 'corn has selected and attached to its human. I'm afraid Nova is bonded to you for good, and that you are both going to fade as long as you are separated." He looked very grave. "Either that, or Gunter's bread was moldy."

Gunter eyed the H.W. coldly, and reached

for his battleaxe.

"But I'm sure it's the attachment thing!" the H.W. added quickly.

Amethyst's eyes widened in fear. "I'm going to die, aren't I?"

"I'm afraid so, little lady, and there's nothing in the world that can prevent it," said the Hoarse Whisperer. Then he added, "But that's nothing to worry about. Everybody dies, you know."

"I mean *soon*," Amethyst said with mounting alarm. "I'm going to die from being separated from Nova!"

The H.W. looked shocked. "Oh, heavens no, child! I don't expect you'll end up with anything worse than a harmless sinus infection from this."

"Considering her sinuses," said Gunter, "I'm not sure that's so harmless."

"I see what you mean," said the Hoarse.

They finished their meal and continued onward.

It wasn't long after they entered the forest that they heard a horse's whinny from up ahead (not a unicorn's whinny—full of sparkles and light—but a normal, everyday I-have-something-I'm-just-dying-to-tell-the-world-but-I-can-only-make-this-one-sound kind of whinny that regular horse's have). The H.W. held a finger to his lips to shush his companions, and the three of them crept slowly toward the source of the sound.

Beside the path was a dense clump of bushes. Amethyst, Gunter, and the H.W. huddled silently behind the greenery and peered through. On the other side of the bushes was a clearing containing three tents, a horse hitched to a wagon, and three people—more or less—around a low campfire. There were no unicorns in sight.

Amethyst recognized one of the fire-sitters as the hunched, eye-patched wagon driver who had visited her farm with Ro-bear the tax collector on the previous Tuesday. He was dressed shabbily, as if a burlap bag had suddenly sprouted a head and eyes—well, one eye, anyway. He was sitting on a log, looking up at a man standing above him.

"Scar and I have been talking, Ralph," said the eye-patched man, "and we'd like to make a suggestion to improve our little group's effectiveness."

The man he had called Ralph stood with one foot resting on a stone, staring dreamily into the distance. He wore a green tunic, a green hat with a feather affixed at a jaunty angle, and green tights. His outfit seemed abnormally clean for a man who lived in the woods. In fact, he looked as if he was posing to have his portrait painted.

"Do tell," said Ralph.

"We want to change our name."

"What!" said Ralph, pulled from his dreamy staring. "The name thing again? Really, One-Eye?"

"I'm telling you, Ralph, a new name could

108

really help us."

"I like the name we've got," said Ralph.

"But we need a name people can get excited about, something that will help us with recruiting other thieves, something that will inspire people. 'Men of Reality' couldn't inspire its way out of a paper sack."

"Besides," said the third person, the one called Scar, "not all of us are men."

From his place behind the bush, Gunter looked at Scar—a roundish, squat sort of ruffian—then back at One-Eye, then at Ralph, to determine which one wasn't a man. He couldn't do it.

"It's too late to change the name," said Ralph. "I've already ordered the business cards and letterhead from Heathrow Payne."

"But we need a name that pushes us toward greatness," insisted One-Eye.

"But that's precisely the point!" said Ralph. "We don't need some marketing department title to make us seem like something we're not. 'Men of Reality' is honest, and we thieves are nothing if not honest. We face facts; we don't need some manufactured feel-good psych-up to do our thing. We can take things as they actually are."

"I wonder what your cousin in England would say," said One-Eye.

"Hmph! My cousin!" snorted Ralph. "What would he know about it?"

"Well, wouldn't you agree he's met with some success—"

"But they're dishonest! 'Rob from the rich

and give to the poor' my foot! He and his 'Merry Men' are rolling in money. And that name of theirs—does anyone really believe they are actually merry? Of course not! It's all a deception, a deliberate manipulation of public image, and everyone knows it."

"But isn't it just possible their name, dishonest as it may be, has contributed at least slightly to their success?" said One-Eye.

"Whatever success they've had is a direct result of their cushy situation." Ralph's anger was clearly rising. "I ask you, what hardships has he ever had to face? He lives in a dry and well-appointed cave in the tranquil-sounding Sherwood Forest with a dozen of his best friends. And don't even get me started on his monarch: a usurping tyrant who is raising political oppression to an art form. All my cousin has to do is drop a clever little slogan here and there, and the public opinion campaign is won. Our situation is totally different. We live in a place called Nightmare Forest, for crying out loud! Our monarch is a puffy-faced, hairless wonder—largely sympathetic to the masses—and only a half-hearted tyrant. How do you make him seem like the bad guy when you steal money for a living? We'd be merry, too, I'd wager, if we had such an easy target as does my cousin. If you were an honest thief, you'd admit that I'm right."

"What you say is true," said One-Eye. "Our situation *is* harder, which is why we need all the help we can get. We need an inspiring name. The only thing 'Men of Reality' inspires me to do is take a nap."

Ralph took a deep breath and let it out slowly. He appeared to be thinking about what One-Eye had said—either that or he was considering taking a nap.

"Okay," Ralph said. "Let's suppose for the sake of argument that we need a new name. Do you have any suggestions?"

One-Eye straightened as if he were about to make a grand announcement. "How do you feel about"—he paused for dramatic effect—"'Ralph Hood and his Self-Actualized Men?'"

"Persons," corrected Scar.

"Uh, yeah," said One-Eye. "Self-Actualized Persons."

Ralph considered this for a moment. "I like the Ralph Hood part," he said, "but the rest of it is awful."

It was at this moment that Amethyst, having stored up all of the sneezing she would ordinarily have done during a conversation of this length, found she could contain herself no longer. She let loose with a blast that split the relative peace of the forest and blew a swirling swarm of leaves from the bush in front of her.

Before our heroes had a chance to stand up and run away, a voice came from behind them: "Hold it right there."

Amethyst, Gunter, and the H. W. slowly raised their hands and turned around to see Scar pointing a keenly sharpened and polished sword at them. Gunter was astonished that one with so much extra baggage around the middle could have moved with such speed. At this close range, Gunter nearly decided that Scar was indeed a female, but then thought, *Nah. It's still a toss-up.*

"Uh, guys?" Gunter muttered to his companions.

"Yes?" said his companions.

"Run!" Gunter shouted as he exploded into motion, bringing his battleaxe crashing down on Scar's sword, nearly knocking it from her (yes, she was indeed a woman) hand. In a dizzying flurry the axe sliced the air again and again, ringing off of the sword, which came up again and again to meet it. The speed and ferocity of each of the fighters was astonishing. First Gunter would advance, then Scar would gain ground. Scar would parry and thrust, Gunter would duck and swing. Back and forth, toe-to-toe they went at it, a masterful display of skill and technique seldom seen before in all of Rondolay. At last, Gunter launched into a blur of flash and clang that left Scar backed helplessly against a tree, her sword on the ground at her feet—

"Enough!" came a shout from behind Gunter. He turned to see Ralph holding Amethyst by the back of her collar. "We wouldn't want any harm to come to the little girl, would we?"

Gunter looked to the H.W., who, in fleeing the scene as fast as his legs would carry him, had made it nearly four feet before One-Eye had captured him.

Gunter, breathless and out of options, realized he was beaten. He bent to pick up Scar's sword and give it back to her. "That's a fine blade you've got there," he said. "Who's your supplier?"

Less than five minutes later, Amethyst, Gunter, and the H.W. were sitting back-to-back in the dirt in the clearing, their hands tied behind them.

"Now," said Ralph, leaning down to look Amethyst menacingly in the eye. "How long were you three hiding behind that bush?"

"Long enough to know you people really need a new name," said Amethyst.

One-Eye turned to Ralph. "See? *See?*"

Ralph rolled his eyes.

"We're here for the lassie's unicorn," said Gunter. "What have you done with him?"

"Unicorn?" said Ralph. "We have no unicorn."

"You did," said the H.W. "I saw you take him. I followed you here."

At the sound of Hoarse's voice, the three thieves looked at each other in shock.

"Sounds like a grindstone working over a bagful of pottery shards," said Ralph.

"Now you see why I live alone," the H.W. said under his breath.

"I know you," said Amethyst to One-Eye. "You work with Robber the tax collector."

"Yes," he said. "I help out the king part-time when he needs flexible staffing options for his tax initiatives. I'm something of a consultant, you might say."

"I might say you're something of a thief," said Amethyst. "You stole my unicorn from me."

"Well......," said Ralph. "Yes. We did. And you have to admit it was a first-rate bit of thievery, too."

"And you have to admit it was mean and terrible and awful and...and...give him back right now!" shouted Amethyst.

"We don't have him anymore," said Ralph. "Check with King Engelbert."

"Wait," said Amethyst. "You mean the king has Nova?"

"Let's just say that when the king heard we had a prime unicorn for sale to the highest bidder, he couldn't wait to reward us for our ingenuity. Isn't that right, Scar?"

"Absolutely," said Scar, holding up a money bag and giving it a jingling shake.

"Then let us go," said Amethyst. "If you don't have Nova then there's no reason for you to hold us."

"The girl's got a point there, Ralph," said Scar. "What are we holding them for?"

"Ransom, of course." Ralph looked exceedingly pleased with himself.

"Oh, the girl's mother doesn't have any money," said One-Eye. "Come to think of it, she doesn't even have any spoons."

"Maybe not," said Ralph, "but that armor the girl and the dwarf are wearing looks valuable. There must be someone in this kingdom willing to pay for these three, if only we can figure out who."

As the thieves discussed their next steps, Gunter whispered to his companions: "What we need is to win one of them over to our side. I've always had a way with the ladies. Watch as I work the old Flintlock magic." He cleared his throat and locked eyes with Scar, who was adding vegetables to a pot hanging over the fire. "I hear tell that one among this fine company is a female," he said, lifting his eyebrows in his most fetching expression. "That wouldn't be you now, would it?"

Scar stared at him for a moment, then, with a quickness and accuracy Gunter wouldn't have believed possible a moment before, ricocheted a half-peeled potato off his forehead.

"Ouch!" shouted Gunter in pain and anger. "Aye! Some people just can't take a compliment!"

The thieves laughed uproariously. One-Eye and Scar high-fived each other.

"Looks like our Scar made quite an *impression* on you," said Ralph. "There's no better shot with a tuber in all the kingdom."

"Look on the bright side," said Amethyst to Gunter. "You're lucky she was making dinner instead of pitching horseshoes."

"If that was an example of the old Flintlock magic," whispered the Hoarse Whisperer, "I'd say it's a wonder you were ever born."

"I'd like to see you do better," said Gunter, wishing desperately that his hands were free so that he could check the size of the bump he could feel growing out of his forehead.

"Okay," rasped the H.W. "I'll see if I can warm them up." He turned his attention to the thieves and said, "Do you like riddles?"

"I do," said One-Eye, "if they're clever."

"Then try this one: Why aren't horses good dancers?"

"Um...because they're animals, and animals don't know how to dance?"

"No," croaked Hoarse. "It's because they have two left feet!" The H.W. burst out in unrestrained laughter.

One-Eye looked confused. "When does the clever part come?"

Ralph looked at Hoarse with warning in his expression. "If you're trying to get on our good side, please stop now."

"Hold on, I've got another one," said Hoarse.

"Threatening us will get you nowhere."

"But this is a really good one."

"I can't wait," said Ralph, his tone indicating that he would have been more than happy to wait, forever if possible.

"A horse walks into a tavern and the bartender says, 'Hey, buddy, why the long face?'—Get it? Looooooong face?"

"To think I nearly had to live out the rest of

my life without having heard that," said Ralph.

One-Eye still looked confused. "Was *that* the clever part?"

"You want I should bean him with a potato?" said Scar.

"No, no," said Ralph. "There's no need to waste our food. We have our swords if he tries it again."

*Escape!*

It was fully dark when the thieves sat down around the fire to eat their supper. Over bowls of stew, they discussed strategies for converting their three captives into some kind of monetary gain, but they could not agree on a satisfactory plan. One-Eye had already made clear that Amethyst's mother had nothing but rhubarb with which to pay a ransom. Though they thought it possible the H.W. might have some money stashed somewhere, the fact that he was a hermit and therefore didn't actually know any people from whom they could demand ransom limited their options severely. Scar said she had heard rumor of a laundress in town who knew him, though, considering his collection of horse jokes, there was some doubt about whether the laundress would pay to get him back.

"Perhaps she would pay us *not* to let him go?" suggested One-Eye.

"Maybe," agreed Ralph, "but then we'd have to keep him with us, and I doubt there's enough gold in the kingdom to make that worthwhile."

The thieves finally agreed their best bet for some quick cash was Gunter, but decided to leave deciding on the next steps until morning.

"Good night, hostages," said Ralph. "Sorry to leave you tied up like that, but we haven't decided what to do with you, and wish to take it up again in the morning when we're fresh. And, please," he said to Amethyst, "try to put the kibosh on the sneezes for the remainder of the night. I'm a remarkably light sleeper."

With that, Ralph, One-Eye, and Scar crawled into their tents and pulled the flaps.

After several minutes, loud snoring was heard coming from all three of the thieves' tents.

"Finally," said the H.W. "The time has come for us to make our move."

"But we *can't* move, Mr. Hoarse," whispered Amethyst. "That's the problem."

"But I've got a plan. It will require split-second timing, nerves of steel, and a chipmunk with an insatiable fondness for chewing."

"Chipmunk with an insatiable...?" began Gunter in disbelief. "Sorry, but I seem to have left all my chipmunks in my other suit of armor."

"Fortunately, I happen to have just such a creature hiding in the front pocket of my robe," said the H.W. He gave a pair of short, low whistles. His pocket vibrated for a moment before a brown, furry blur streaked from his pocket up onto his shoulder. "Meet my Secret Weapon."

Gunter turned his head over his shoulder to look and was confronted by a close-up of little black eyes like beads of shiny onyx set on each side of a freakishly large set of yellow buck teeth.

"Whoa!" gasped Gunter. "You could scrape paint off a barn with those things."

"His name is Fang," said the H.W. "As you can see, he has a nearly terrifying capacity for incisor growth."

"You can say that again," said Gunter.

"He's constantly gnawing to grind his teeth down. He's brilliant—for a rodent. I spent the last two months teaching him to chew on command."

"He's adorable," said Amethyst.

"Aye," said Gunter, "in a hideous kind of way."

"Chew, Fang," said the H.W. "Go on, boy, chew the ropes."

Almost quicker than the eye could track, Fang hopped onto Gunter and perched on his shoulder. His fuzzy little head (Fang's, not Gunter's) flicked right and left as if to make sure the thieves were still in their tents.

"Good boy, Fang," said the H.W. "Go ahead. Chew."

Without the slightest sound, the heroic little rodent disappeared behind Gunter's back.

"Good boy," whispered Gunter, smiling broadly. "Good boy, Fang-uh-uh-UH!" Gunter's eyes grew wide as he began to jerk and twitch like a man having a seizure. "The rope! The rope, you ridiculous rodent! Leave my pants alone!"

Frightened by Gunter's thrashing, Fang darted out onto Gunter's thigh, and emitted a series of sharp gibbering sounds at the dwarf that could only have been a chipmunk's version of a severe scolding. The chipmunk gave Gunter a final, withering glare, then darted off into the woods.

"Fang! Come back! Come back!" whispered the Hoarse Whisperer.

"Taught him to chew on command, eh?" said Gunter. "I wish you had taught him to chew on ropes!"

Amethyst watched the spot where the little creature had disappeared into the darkness. "Will he be coming back, then?" she said.

"Probably not," admitted the H.W.

"Maybe he's just gone for help?" said Amethyst, hopefully.

"I'm thinking no," said the H.W. "I don't think he was really all that happy living with me, anyway."

"So," said Gunter, "we'll be moving on to other escape plans that don't involve waiting for disproportionately endowed rodents to materialize out of the woods to save us?"

"Yes. Definitely," said the H.W., working to compose himself. Though he was trying not to show it, he was more than a little hurt at the betrayal by the Secret Weapon.

"Is there a back-up plan?" asked Gunter. "Maybe one requiring split-second timing, nerves of steel, and something *other* than a chipmunk with an insatiable fondness for chewing?"

"Um...no," replied the H.W. "I've got nothing."

As they sat without speaking, pondering their options, all three became aware of the sound of something creeping slowly toward them through the underbrush beyond the firelight.

"What is that, Mr. Flintlock?" said Amethyst.

"I'm not sure, lass," said Gunter, straining to see. "But whatever it is, it's a good deal larger than a buck-toothed chipmunk." As Gunter peered into the darkness, a figure emerged from the shadows, walking on two legs, clanking a little, and casting off warbly reflections of orange firelight.

It was a knight in shining armor.

Gunter began to say, "Here's hoping you're not a Self-Actualized Person," but the knight lifted a single, gauntleted finger in front of his face shield.

"Shhhhhhhh," came an echoey shushing sound from inside the knight's helmet. He moved past our heroes without another glance, busying himself near the three tents. He moved remarkably quietly for a person encased entirely in sheet metal.

"What's he doing?" the Hoarse Whisperer whispered hoarsely.

Only Amethyst could see what the knight was doing, though she didn't understand the purpose of most of it. "I can't tell," she whispered back. "Something with some ropes from the cart, I think."

After nearly 20 minutes, the suit of armor walked back to Amethyst, Gunter, and the H.W., and, with another silent shushing motion, cut the ropes that bound them. Gunter retrieved his battleaxe, Amethyst's dagger, and the H.W.'s riding crop, and silently followed the knight in the night back the way he had come through the underbrush. They continued without speaking for some distance, the H.W. massaging his wrists where the rope had bound them, and Gunter checking to make sure Fang's chewing hadn't left him with a hole in his pants.

Just at that moment, with the remarkably coincidental timing of a thinly veiled plot device, Amethyst fired off another of her trademark sneezes. It shattered the nighttime silence and spooked a flock of doves that were sleeping in the trees above.

Ralph, hearing the sneeze (he was, after all, a remarkably light sleeper) and realizing his prisoners were escaping, shouted his colleagues awake and burst from his tent, still trying to thread his second foot into the first leg of his green leggings. Though he was instantly aware that his hoped-for ransom was rapidly disappearing into the trees, he was not aware that the knight had placed snare traps[†††] outside each of the

---

[†††] A snare trap is an Improvised Anti-Personnel Mechanism consisting of a loop of rope attached to the top of an evergreen or other youngish tree that has been bent downward to make a sort of natural spring. When the snare is tripped by someone or some thing stepping inside the loop, the tree snaps upward in an effort to return to its original shape, and the rope loop instantly tightens around whatever is inside it, hauling the tripee into the air by his (or, in Scar's case, possibly *her*) ankles. You've undoubtedly seen this type of trap in movies or

three tents before freeing the captives.

Upon leaving their tents, Ralph, One-Eye, and Scar found their worlds spinning crazily with pine needles whapping them from all sides as they bobbed up and down in mid-air. It took some moments before Ralph was able to piece together what had happened to him, and that his two companions were also hanging upside down 20 feet off the ground. The last sound he heard from his former hostages was laughter fading in the distance. Ralph was sure they were laughing at him.

---

cartoons, and they are an exceedingly convenient way of putting Bad Guys out of commission in a way that also tends to add some comic relief to a story line, usually after a tense situation. They are also good for preventing the Bad Guys from pursuing the Good Guys as they leave the tense situation. When the trees used are sufficiently thick and tall, as they were in this case (the knight had used the cart horse to help supplement his tree-bending weight), they might even hoist the Bad Guys sufficiently high into the air as to prevent them from showing up at all in the remainder of the story, except perhaps for a mention in the odd footnote or side discussion later on at the castle. Fortunately for Ralph and his companions, they were left hanging above the reach of any passing bears or mountain lions that might otherwise have engaged in a frenzied game of "tether-thief." Snares are such convenient plot devices, in fact, that it struck me that you, Dear Reader, might think I have stuck them in at this point for the sake of my own personal ease without regard to their plausibility or the engineering required to make them work. But let me assure you that such is not the case. Fortunately for all involved, the knight had taken an entire semester of "Improvised Anti-Personnel Mechanisms" at Knight School. And let me just say I'm glad he did, too, because those trusty ole snare traps were just what the story needed at this point.

The last thing Amethyst heard from her former captors was Ralph's voice screaming some ways behind her: "Some band of Self-Actualized Persons! We've just been overwhelmed by a little girl, a geriatric dwarf, and a laryngitic monk!"[‡‡‡]

---

[‡‡‡] In case you are the sort of person who worries about people left hanging around in trees—even if they are Bad Guys— I should mention what happened to Ralph, One-Eye, and Scar. After the Improvised Anti-Personnel Mechanisms had rendered them harmless, the thieves continued to hang upside down 20 feet above the ground for more than a week, at which point they were rescued by a brave little tailor who had wandered into Nightmare Forest from another fairytale. The Self-Actualized Persons, mistaking him for the wealthy shoemaker who had been helped by the elves, showed their gratitude by attempting to hold him for ransom. This effort failed when a bucktoothed chipmunk scampered out of the forest and chewed through the ropes that bound the tailor, allowing him to escape. When confronted with this latest failure, Ralph Hood suspected it was somehow the fault of his cousin in England.

A hundred yards down the path, Amethyst and her friends suddenly realized their rescuer was no longer walking alongside them. They stopped and looked back to where the suit of armor was standing motionless in the moonlight.

"That...was...AWESOME!" shouted the armor, leaping from the ground in a burst of joy that would have been truly impressive if the 90 pounds of sheet metal hadn't constrained it to more of a sad, tottering hop. Then the suit of armor began jigging around in a clumsy, clanking dance while a procession of laughter began inside the helmet that Amethyst was certain could have wakened the dead.

"Shhhh!!!!" Amethyst shushed the knight in alarm. "I don't wish to seem ungrateful for the rescue, Mr. Knight," she said, "and I'm really glad you're enjoying our moonlight escape, but shouldn't we be fleeing with all possible haste? What if they come after us?"

"Not much chance of that," said the suit of armor, ending his laughter and tottering to a stop. "In Knight School, I wasn't much at full frontal assaults, but I was top of my class in Improvised Anti-Personnel Mechanisms."

"So who have we to thank for our rescue?" said Gunter.

The knight lifted his visor for a moment and peeked out. "It is I, Timmy the Tremulous," came the thin, cracking voice. He snapped the visor shut again.

"Timmy!" exclaimed Amethyst. "What are you doing here? You said you were terrified of open spaces!"

"That I am, and I must admit it had me beaten at first. There was no way I was leaving the relative safety of my dish-tub for an outdoor quest. But I kept thinking about what you said, and finally I realized I had the answer standing in my broom closet."

"Why were you standing in your broom closet?" asked the H.W.

*"I* wasn't standing in my broom closet," said the helmet, shaking back and forth. *"The answer* was standing in my broom closet. This"—the suit of armor banged loudly on its own chest—"is the answer. My armor. I'm sealed up in a tin can. Being completely encased in metal isn't what anyone would call wide open spaces."

"Aye," said Gunter with more than a little admiration in his voice. "You're as safe as a wee can of Vienna sausage."

"Exactly!" said the helmet. "And it offers far better protection against falling boulders than a thatched roof. I may take to wearing it from now on, even indoors."

"How clever!" said Amethyst. "I'm so glad you found a way! I knew you could do it!"

In her exuberance, she lunged to hug Timmy around the waist, but only succeeded in tipping him off balance. He stumbled backward, tripped over a rock, and toppled noisily into a patch of poison sumac.

"Oh," said Amethyst, sheepishly. "Sorry about that."

"Think nothing of it, fair damsel," said Timmy, struggling to roll onto his hands and knees and crawl out of the brush. "Though perhaps next time you could give a little warning. The helmet makes it harder to see what's coming at me."

"Brain Can™ helmets are known for that," said Gunter. "You should get a Head Cage™. They're much better. I can get you a discount on one back at the Maul."

"I'll try to keep that in mind," said Timmy, "but for now I'm just hoping the thing doesn't come off." He climbed again to his feet and plucked a wad of poison sumac from the corner of his helmet visor. "My main problem now is I think I'm developing claustrophobia."

"You're kidding!" said Amethyst.

"Actually, yes, I am," said Timothy, and she could tell from the sound of his voice that he was smiling behind his faceplate.

The four of them resumed walking.

"How did you ever find us?" croaked the H.W.

"It wasn't hard," said Timmy. "You told us back at the Rent-a-Rogue that the quest was in Nightmare Forest, and Amethyst's sneezes can be heard for at least a mile. I just homed in on the sneezes and then hid in the brush until the

128

ruffians had retired for the night. Only, unless it was masterfully disguised, I didn't see any ponies back there."

"Yeah...," began Amethyst, coolly. "About that—"

Gunter interrupted: "That was a fine piece of rescuing back there, Timmy. You really saved our giblets. I didn't think you had it in you."

"Well thank you, good sir," said Timmy. "Strategic Planning and Battlefield Trickery was my favorite class at Knight School."

"You went to Knight School? The rental agent didn't mention that," said Gunter.

"That's because I didn't graduate," said Timmy. "It's quite embarrassing, really. I've wanted to be a hero ever since I was a little kid. My father gave me a wooden sword and shield one Christmas. I spent most of that spring on a death-defying quest to vanquish the family cow."

"You vanquished a cow?" said Gunter.

"Sure," said Timmy. "In my experience, people have badly underestimated the potential value of the bovine in warfare simulations. I rode off to the Crusades on her, too. But my favorite game was rescuing the damsel in distress—"

"Don't tell me," said the H.W. between wheezes—he was struggling to keep up with Timmy's excited pace. "The cow."

"Well," admitted Timmy, becoming suddenly concerned that he had revealed too much, too soon. "I didn't have any sisters."

"You were a lonely child, weren't you, lad?"

asked Gunter.

"What makes you say that?" said Timmy.

"Lucky guess," said Gunter.

"Oh. Anyway, when I finally got into Knight School, I was thrilled. My parents were proud. We had a party with all the relatives. I loved being part of that school. But all that changed one morning."

"What happened?" asked Amethyst.

"Remember my fear of open spaces? Well, we had a class on broadsword handling that met in an open area outside the main building. One morning about two months into my second year, I got so nervous—I told you how my hands sweat, right?"

They nodded.

"Well, we were practicing our full overhead swings,"—he raised one arm and began moving his hand in circles in the air—"the move they call the 'hair razor.'"

"Aye, laddie!" said Gunter—though, since Gunter often rolled his "r"s, it was indistinguishable from the way he would have pronounced the name Larry. "I love that move."

"Well," continued Timmy, "just as I was working up to maximum velocity, the broadsword slipped out of my hand, swung wildly across the courtyard, and pinned the headmaster's plumed hat to the wall behind him. He was so angry, he just stood there twitching and jerking, groping at the top of his head to make sure he hadn't lost anything important. The more he clutched at his hair, the redder his face became. There might still have been some hope for me until I made the mistake of suggesting it probably felt far worse than it looked, and that the bald stripe in the middle would undoubtedly grow back in three or four months, tops. I was expelled before lunchtime. That's why they were only asking 13 gold pieces for me at the Rent-a-Rogue. It's embarrassing, really."

"Well, you needn't be embarrassed about that any longer, laddie," said Gunter with high regard in his voice. "After your performance in the Rescue of Nightmare Forest, your price will be going up. I'll see to it personally."

It was quite late when the little band of adventurers reached Amethyst's farm. Amethyst's mother was so surprised to see the strange collection of characters who followed her daughter into the kitchen/bedroom/dinette that she completely forgot to scold the girl for being out so late and worrying her half to death.

"We're back, Mother," said Amethyst (for she was the only one whose mother was there).

"Amethyst!" said Amethyst's mother. "What has happened to you? You look ill. Why are you home so late?" And then, almost as an afterthought, "Why are you wearing gnome armor?"

"How did you know it's gnome armor?" said Amethyst.

"When one is a rhubarb farmer, one needs

131

a hobby."

"Oh. Mother, I'd like you to meet my friends: this is Gunter the Arms Dealer, Timmy the Agoraphobic Knight, and the Hoarse Whisperer. Is it okay if they spend the night in the barn?"

"You and your strays...," began Amethyst's mother. "No, sweetie, I'm afraid you can't keep them. How much do you think three grown men eat?"

"They're not strays, Mother," said Amethyst. "They're helping me get Nova back."

"You are?" Amethyst's mother addressed the three men. "Well, thank you so much for your efforts, gentlemen. Remarkable the trouble a little girl with a pack of crayons can stir up."

"Oh, it is no trouble, Ma'am," volunteered Timmy. "It is a pleasure to help such a determined and inspiring young lady."

"Besides," agreed Gunter, "'tisn't every day one gets a chance to see a real live mythical creature."

"Why, thank you," said Amethyst's mother, blushing slightly.

"I think he was talking about Nova, Mother," said Amethyst.

"Have I missed something?" said Timmy. "What's so mythical about a lost pony?"

Amethyst quizzed Gunter and the H.W. with her eyes. She had decided to tell Timmy about Nova—he had earned that much—but she wondered about the best way to tell him he had

132

risked his life for something most people didn't believe existed. What if he didn't believe her? What if he felt like they had tricked him? What if he got mad?

"Nova is a unicorn," she said flatly.

"Oh," said Timmy. "No wonder you want him back so badly."

Amethyst exchanged another set of glances with Gunter and the H.W.

"You don't find it hard to believe that Nova is a unicorn?" asked Gunter.

"The damsel is always right—at least, that's what they told me in Knight School," said Timmy. "They also told me to remember my place; knights provide rescues, not therapy. But I have a feeling I can trust Amethyst on this one. So where is he? I didn't see him at the rescue."

"The king has him," croaked the H.W. "The thieves sold him to Engelbert before we got there."

At the sound of the H.W.'s voice, Amethyst's mother looked alarmed and quickly moved to put a pot on the fire.

"Oh, you poor dear," she said. "I'll have some tea for you in a jiffy. Sorry if it's a bit weak; we haven't had a new teabag in a couple of years."

"Have you a lemon wedge to add to it?" said Hoarse.

"Well, yes," replied Amethyst's mother, "but it's even older than the teabag."

"In that case, never mind."

"Since you are helping Amethyst," said

133

Amethyst's mother, "you may certainly spend the night in the barn. Nova's stall is available. And we still have some boiled rhubarb left from dinner, if anyone is hungry."

"I pass," the three men said in unison.

"First we should sit down and discuss our strategy for attacking the palace tomorrow," said Amethyst.

"Yes," said Amethyst's mother, "do sit down and discuss...attacking...the...palace? Amethyst, is there something you need to tell me?"

"I'm not so sure storming a fortified castle with just the four of us is such a good idea," said Gunter as they took their seats around the kitchen/dinette table. "There is an entire garrison of soldiers quartered in there."

"Entire garrison...?" said Amethyst's mother.

"Oh, I don't think we'll need any castle storming to get the little unicorn back," said the H.W.

"Well, I'd call that a relief," said Gunter. "There was a time I would have been up for it, but I wouldn't try it now without another three or four men. I'm not as young as I used to be, you know."

"You can say that again," said the H.W.

Gunter shot him a good-natured sneer.

"I don't think any of that will be necessary," continued Hoarse. "Unless I miss my guess, I'm pretty sure the king will be glad to see Amethyst by the time we get there."

"Why is that?" said Amethyst.

"Attachment issues. Remember I told you that the sicker you get, the sicker Nova will get? By the time we reach the castle I think it will be obvious even to King Engelbert that the two of you mustn't be separated any longer."

Amethyst felt quite sick by the time they set out for town the next day. Her face was horribly pale with dark spots developing like bruises under her eyes.

Amethyst's mother handed them each a limp stalk of rhubarb for the road, and waved goodbye to them from the farmhouse doorway. Her face showed some worry about her daughter's physical state. She would not have allowed Amethyst to leave the house if the hooded stranger with the voice like a meat grinder choking on broken glass hadn't assured her that Amethyst was fine for traveling and that all would soon be well.

Amethyst stumbled along in uncharacteristic silence, her head bowed as though it took all of her concentration to keep her feet moving in sequence. She had left her gnome armor at home.

Inside the castle's high outer wall was a courtyard that swarmed with palace staff going about their duties. Some were engaged in various maintenance activities, pushing wheelbarrows of stones (holding, not made of) toward a half-finished structure, others pushing wheelbarrows containing something else away from the Royal Stables.

In the center of all this activity, King

Engelbert stood motionless, draped in Royal Robes and holding a Royal Scepter aloft in one hand. Nearby, Queen Arabella was snipping furiously at a tall piece of garden shrubbery with a dangerous-looking pair of hedge trimmers. Every few moments she would interrupt her clipping, study her husband, compare his shape with that of the foliage in front of her, then attack the bush again with renewed vigor. So far her project looked remarkably like a leafy Statue of Liberty.

"Raise the scepter higher, dear," she said cheerfully. "You're sagging."

The king lifted his hand a few inches then reset the look of determined nobility on his face.

Outside the wall, Amethyst, Gunter, the H.W., and Timmy stood at the castle's imposing wooden gate. Gunter rapped several times on the thick timbers with his axe handle. Above them, a small window high in the gate opened, and the face of a palace guard appeared in it.

"Who goes there?" said the face.

"It is the lass Amethyst," Gunter said boldly, "come seeking an audience with King Engelbert on a matter of great importance." His tone was grander than usual; the situation seemed to call for it.

The guard looked down at them doubtfully. "Does she have an appointment?"

"Uh...no," said Gunter.

"Are you some kind of envoy from a foreign power?"

"Uh...no," Gunter said again, the boldness draining from his voice.

"You don't look like anybody from the Royal List of Approved Suppliers."

"Actually, I've been trying to get on that," said Gunter, deftly sticking a fragment of leather onto the tip of his ax and lifting it up to the guard. "Here's my card. Gunter Flintlock, armaments and weaponry, at your service."

The guard took the "card" and eyed it skeptically. "You're peddlers, then?" he said.

"Well, not today, no," answered Gunter.

"Beggars?"

"No."

"An itinerant troupe of wandering troubadours?"

Gunter looked his companions up and down. "Not even close."

"Traveling acrobats, then?"

"Nope."

"We aren't making much progress here, are we?" said the guard.

Gunter looked at Hoarse and Timmy for help.

"Keep going," whispered Timmy. "You're doing great."

At that, Amethyst looked up at the guard for the first time, tipping her head back to reveal a drawn, pale face with dark circles beneath her eyes.

"I say," said the guard. "She doesn't look at all well. She doesn't have the plague, does she?

Perhaps sent here by Tarnation to infect the Royal Family?"

"She doesn't have the plague," said Gunter.

"What's so important, then?"

"It's private," said Gunter. "For the king's ears only."

"Is that right? The king's ears only? If I had a gold piece for every beggar that came to these gates with a sob story about why it was a moral imperative that he see the king, well...I'd have more than one gold piece, I can tell you." Then he addressed Amethyst: "So please tell me, little waif, what's so important that a tattered dishrag such as yourself *demands* to speak with the Royal Monarch of the entire nation of Rondolay?"

Amethyst had had enough. She had lost her pet, launched a public awareness campaign, evaded the Cogs of Doom, recruited help, been taken captive, escaped, and walked goodness-knew how many miles—*and* had maintained a polite and positive outlook throughout. But she was done now. She had started out with a broken heart, and had since added exhaustion and illness to it. All at once, it became quite clear to Amethyst that she had endured enough. It was about to become clear to everyone else, as well.

Amethyst locked eyes with the guard and said slowly, with building volume: "He. Has. My. UNICORN!"

At the sound of the word "UNICORN," the queen, who had been working at the armpit of her masterpiece, slipped badly with the trimmers.

*Snip!*

The shrub's raised arm separated from the sculpture and dropped without celebration to the ground at her feet.

"Oh dear," she said, looking startled and perplexed. "I guess you can put your arm down now."

She looked at King Engelbert. An expression of shock had taken over his Royal Face.

"Did I just hear the word 'unicorn'?" he asked.

"I believe you did," said the queen.

"Excuse me a moment." Engelbert dropped his scepter in the grass and ran—as best as he was able in the Royal Robes—toward the gate.

Amethyst was still looking at the castle guard's face framed in the little doorway when his head was suddenly pushed aside and replaced by another, puffier face with penciled-in eyebrows. The face looked them up and down for a moment before it spoke.

"Congratulations, little girl!" said King Engelbert, a little too enthusiastically. "You used today's secret password!"

"Secret password?" said Amethyst. "What secret password?"

"Why, I can't tell you, of course—it's a secret! If one goes around all day repeating the secret password, one can hardly expect it to remain secret now, can one? But you used it! And today only, my dear, using that special word that I'm not going to repeat gets you immediate entrance into the castle and a special meeting with me, the king. So hold on, don't go anywhere! And, please, don't speak anymore—wouldn't want you overusing that password!"

The face disappeared and the little window closed. After a few moments, one of the massive gate doors swung open and our heroes saw a pair of guards inside, beckoning them to enter.

Amethyst dragged herself in, followed by Gunter, Timmy, and the H.W. The king was nowhere to be seen.

"You will follow us, please," said the guard from the gate, now smiling broadly as he turned with the other guard to lead Amethyst and her friends across the courtyard. While they were walking, he turned to the second guard and said in a low voice, "Did you know we had a secret password?"

# The King Wants Answers

The group walked through the courtyard, up some stone steps, and into one of the castle's outbuildings. The room was large, half-filled with sealed barrels, piles of hay and straw, and buckets of oats. Horse halters and reins hung in rows along the walls.

The king and queen were already there, sitting side by side on an oblong wooden box.

Ro-bear the tax collector was also there, standing sentry just inside the door. "Your Royal Highnesses," he announced importantly, "may I present the peasant girl Amethyst and...uh..."—he gave Gunter, Timmy, and the H.W. a puzzled look—"those with her!"

"Oh, *there* you are!" said King Engelbert as though he had misplaced the four friends earlier in the day and had spent all the time since looking for them. He motioned them to a bench against one wall. "Sit down, sit down, please."

The king nodded to the two guards, who ducked back outside and closed the door, which Ro-bear quickly barred with a thick beam on the inside. It suddenly became very clear to Amethyst and her friends that they would not be leaving that way.

The king's smile vanished.

"Now," he said, rising to his feet and approaching Amethyst, "you will tell me all I want to know. Who told you I have a unicorn?"

"Ralph Hood of Nightmare Forest," said Amethyst without the slightest indication of intimidation.

"And what would make that rapscallion tell a little girl a thing like that," asked the king, "particularly after the sizable sum I paid him and his Men of Reality to keep it to themselves?"

"Self-Actualized Persons."

"What?"

"They call themselves Self-Actualized Persons now," said Amethyst. "They said 'Men of Reality' couldn't inspire anybody to crawl out of a paper bag."

King Engelbert stopped short, his train of thought completely derailed. "Well, I can't argue with that," he said, "mostly because I have no idea what you're talking about."

The queen decided to jump in at that point, mostly in hopes of keeping the interrogation from turning into an all-day ordeal. "Young lady," she said pleasantly, "perhaps you should begin at the beginning and end with the...well, the part we've gotten to so far."

So that's what Amethyst did. She began with wilted rhubarb and wild strawberries, then moved on to baby unicorns, cups of milk, and part-time tax collectors with eye patches. She recounted the mystery of the hooded figure in the mist, the shock of Nova's disappearance, and the strain of the public awareness initiative. She told about meeting Gunter, not meeting the Cogs of Doom, and more than either the king or queen ever wanted to know about the Mystical Beast Protection League, beef-eating minotaurs, and the relative effectiveness of various treatments for agoraphobia. She finished her tale with the details of Nightmare Forest, the public image worries of thieves, the dental problems of rodents, and a Knight in Shining Armor.

When Amethyst finally came to the end of her story, King Engelbert was silent for a long time, thoughtfully rubbing a patch of chin hair that kind of freaked Amethyst out because it seemed to be peeling away from his face in one spot.

"Ah," said the king at last, "the imaginings of children. Penguins, indeed!" He began laughing softly to himself in a way that made it clear he didn't believe a single one of the many words she had said.

The queen, Ro-bear, Amethyst, Gunter, the H.W., and Timmy watched him in silence until his laughter became self-conscious and awkward, then died out altogether.

"You don't mean to tell me you all believe her?" said the king.

At this point, Gunter stood and bowed low to the king.

"My King," he said, "I have been with the lass the longest of any in this company, and though I have not yet seen a unicorn in our travels, I can testify to the truth of the parts of her story where I was present, and I believe her for the parts where I was not. The lass is made of uncommon stuff, and her courage and selfless devotion have surpassed those of many an adult in your kingdom. I can say with full confidence, Your Highness, that, if you believe yourself in possession of a unicorn, I believe it was stolen from Amethyst."

"Here! Here!" shouted the suit of armor, jumping noisily to its feet.

"Dear me!" said the queen, placing her hand over her heart, "you startled me!"

"Oh, sorry, Highness," came Timmy's voice from inside the helmet. He lowered himself awkwardly back onto the bench and added, "But I do agree."

"Unless I miss my guess," rasped the Hoarse Whisperer, "the little unicorn is failing rapidly by now."

The king turned a serious and somewhat puzzled expression toward the queen, who returned it. He turned back to the H.W.

"How did you know that?" he challenged.

"Unicorns attach to people," answered the H.W. "No, I said that wrong—not people—*person*, a single, special person who it selects and bonds to as a sort of soul mate. It's what they are made to do."

"Um," said the king, looking from face to face. He wasn't getting it. "So?"

"If the unicorn is separated from the one he has chosen, he will become sick. The 'corn's decline will continue until he is either reunited with his chosen person or...."

"Or what?" demanded King Engelbert.

The H.W. formed a cutting motion with one finger across the front of his throat and made the customary accompanying sound, which, incredibly, sounded even worse than his normal voice. "The unicorn dies."

Engelbert considered this.

"So you're saying my unicorn has attached to someone who isn't me, and that's why he's sick, because he's separated from"—he glanced at Amethyst—"that person."

"You got it, Kingy," said the H.W.

"And you're sure of this?"

"Well," admitted the H.W., "to be perfectly honest, there isn't a large body of peer-reviewed research on this phenomenon, almost certainly due to the fact that unicorns are only infinitesimally more common than hen's teeth, which don't exist at all."

"So how can you be so sure? What if you aren't any better at diagnosing unicorn ailments than you are at hexing opposing armies?"

"In my own defense, Sire, I would point out that I never said I was a wizard—it was all hearsay and local gossip—"

"Never mind that. We're talking about my unicorn right now—"

"Forgive my boldness, Your Highness," came Timmy's voice from inside the suit of armor, which rose to its feet and then, shuddering unsteadily, bowed deeply and returned upright again. "Timmy the Tremulous, Sire, at your service."

"And?" said the king.

"I do not wish to offend you, oh Sagacious Monarch, but I believe I owe my king the truth, and the truth is he isn't *your* unicorn. You seem to be the only person in this entire tale who hasn't realized that. Nova belongs to this girl. She knows it. Her mother knows it. The thieves who stole it from her know it. And, most importantly of all, the *unicorn* knows it. Nova needs this girl. With her, he will thrive again if we are not too late. Apart from her, he will die." Timmy paused to let what he had said soak in, which was probably a good idea considering his audience. "So, the real question is this: how is the little guy doing?"

That appeared to hit a nerve.

"Well," said King Engelbert, rubbing his chin thoughtfully, "that certainly puts an unexpected turn on things. Ralph Hood did not tell me he had stolen the creature. What's the kingdom coming to when you can't even trust a band of professional thieves to be honest with you?"

He stood up and crossed slowly to a wooden door at the back of the room.

"You must all understand that what I am about to show you is a state secret," the king said gravely. "The outcome of a Royal War depends on keeping this from the enemy. You must not disclose what you are about to see under pain of death."

He pushed the door open.

"Come along, little girl," said King

Engelbert. "Come see your unicorn."

*Reunion*

Outside the little door was a tiny barnyard that ranked higher on the International Livestock Comfort Scale than any other barnyard in the entire medieval world. A high stone wall surrounded it so that no one from outside could see in. A uniform row of sharp spikes stood along the top of the wall to discourage anyone from climbing up the outside and peeking in. There was a large patch of grass, perfectly edged and uniformly trimmed to three inches in height, with matching patches of dandelion and clover. There were piles of straw and new-looking feed boxes holding heaps of hay and sweet grain. A stone trough caught a flow of running water that poured like a graceful fountain from a spout in the wall.

In the middle of all this was a patch of mud where lay a filthy, sickly-looking baby unicorn.

"Nova!" shouted Amethyst, running to him and falling on her knees to hug his neck.

The little unicorn lifted his head slightly, recognition in his eyes, then lowered it again. But he didn't take his eyes—the one on top, anyway—off of Amethyst.

She was shocked at how quickly he had declined. He looked withered. Even his withers looked withered. The general impression of *betterness* so common among unicorns had faded to a projection somewhere south of the barest mediocrity. He was frighteningly thin and caked with mud, and even his lustrous horn seemed to have lost its inner glow.

"Oh, my boy," said Amethyst, cradling his head and beginning to cry, "what have they done to you?"

"We haven't done anything to him," the king blurted, looking defensively at the others who had followed him into the yard. "We've fed and watered and groomed him. We've done everything we could think of to help him, but he just keeps getting weaker."

"I'll be ballywonkled," said Gunter, standing in amazed wonder. "A real unicorn...."

"He has faded badly despite your best efforts," said the H.W. to the king. "Mystical beasts such as unicorns are like hermit crabs: you really shouldn't take one home unless you know how to care for it."

"Well, we did everything we could think of," said King Engelbert, "but he just keeps flopping down there in the mud."

As Nova looked at Amethyst, it seemed to her that the pained look had begun to fade from his eye. In its place, a look that was familiar to Amethyst flickered back to life: peace, calmness, and that strong, self-assured *competence.* She sensed that, on some deep level of his insides, Nova had begun to smile—if such a thing were possible for a unicorn. After a few moments, Nova let out a deep sigh and closed his eyes to rest.

"Don't worry, Your Highness," Amethyst

said through the tears that were running down her face. "Everything is going to be okay now that we're together again."

"The Whisperer was right," said Gunter to the king. "You must let the unicorn go home with the lass."

"You're out of your minds," said the king, "if you think I'm going to take a mystical beast whose presence at the upcoming Twenty-Seventh Battle of Humongus Magnolius will assure victory for our people, and give him to a little girl two social classes below 'peasant' simply because you four say I should."

"Let's not be too hasty," the queen interrupted.

"Why," said King Engelbert. "Did you have something else in mind, my dear?"

"Well, I'm just wondering," Queen Arabella said mysteriously, "if there mightn't be another way...."

It was late afternoon when Robber rode up in the Royal Tax Collection Wagon with an assistant[§§§] beside him. Amethyst's mother emerged from the dilapidated farmhouse doorway, drying a bundle of rhubarb on the dishrag part of her dress.

"Dear me, is it Tuesday again already?" said Amethyst's mother.

---

[§§§] Not One-Eye, though, as no one at the castle had been able to find him.

"No, dear woman, it isn't," said Ro-bear. He stood up in the front of the wagon, unrolled an official-looking scroll, cleared his throat importantly, and read, in his most impressive voice:

By Royal Decree of

# Engelbert, King of Rondolay...

You, Dear Woman, and your daughter,
Amethyst the Allergic, hereafter known as

# Keeper

of the

# Official Secret Weapon
# of the Realm,

are hereby requested to abandon these premises and
come live as guests of the king, for the foreseeable
future, in the Royal Castle, where you will be
paid a small but living wage as

# Mother of the Keeper

of the

# Official Secret Weapon
# of the Realm,

and where the Keeper of the Official
Secret Weapon has already picked out a
color scheme for your rooms there.

Amethyst's mother stood staring, mouth open, and did not move to catch the clump of rhubarb when it fell from her hands into a mud puddle.

A few hours later, Amethyst's mother, still in a healthy state of shock, arrived at the castle. She brought her cutting board and knife in case she had misunderstood and was actually expected to work in the Royal Kitchen. She also brought along her small wooden bowl and the cracked teacup, just in case she still had to pay taxes while at the castle. At first she had been anxious about leaving Massey Fergusson, Petunia the cow, and Clawed the cat unattended, but Ro-bear had quickly volunteered to have members of the Royal Guard care for them while she and Amethyst were away.

"My gracious!" said Amethyst's mother, staring bug-eyed at the multitude of colorful gowns jammed into the wooden wardrobe in her bedroom. "How many people live in this room?"

"Just one, Mother," said Amethyst[****], smiling broadly. "You. My room is the next one over."

"Well, why are all these clothes in here?" asked Amethyst's mother. "Is this the only closet

[****] Amethyst was well on her way to wellness by then. The dark spots under her eyes had vanished, and, though she was still a bit pale, her usual energy and relentless optimism had returned in full.

in the castle?"

"No, Mother. Those are for you to wear. I was able to negotiate several perks for us once the king realized he needed me to keep Nova healthy."

"These are for me?" asked Amethyst's mother.

"For you, Mother. And you deserve every last one of them."

"I don't know what I shall do having so many. Do you mean I'll have to choose which clothes to put on every morning? How do people function having to make so many decisions?"

"I'm sure you'll manage," said Amethyst. "You may even come to like it."

"Perhaps," said Amethyst's mother. "But I shall have to keep my old dress—at least the dishrag part—so I have something to dry my hands on—and what's that thing over there?"

"That's a bed, Mother," said Amethyst. "You sleep on it. There's one for each of us."

The interchange continued this way for at least a half-hour, during which time Amethyst's mother learned about the trials and troubles of castle life—or at least as much as Amethyst could tell her after having lived there for nearly nine hours.

Though the prospect of sleeping on silk sheets in a canopied bed in a fortified castle as a guest of the Royal Family would have dazzled most eight-year-old girls, Amethyst decided to spend the night in the mud. She covered Nova with a blanket (not silk) and laid down next to him so he could feel that she was there with him even while he was asleep.

Gunter and Timmy had departed at some point during the day, though Amethyst had been so overwhelmed by the burst of activity swirling around her that she couldn't have said exactly when they left or where they went. The H.W., however, being the newly appointed *Assistant to the Keeper of the Official Secret Weapon of the Realm*, and being a hermit with no particular reason to go home anyway, had stayed with her. He had taken up residence in the storage/interrogation room next to Nova's yard so that someone would always be with the unicorn. The ancient hermit had spent the night almost asleep on an impossibly hard bench next to a huge basket of rolled oats.

By morning, Nova appeared to be the recipient of a miracle. When Amethyst awakened and pulled the blanket off of him, the little unicorn climbed to his hooves and high-stepped—though a bit wobbly at first—toward the firmer ground of the grass patch. Once there, he shook his dirt-clumped mane and let loose a sunshine/laughter/sparkle whinny such as only a unicorn convincingly on the mend could have produced.

At that moment the supply room door opened and the H.W. stuck his head into the barnyard. "Well, somebody sounds to be feeling better," he croaked cheerfully. "And a delivery boy is here with the wild strawberries and rhubarb you requested."

At the mention of strawberries and rhubarb, Nova's eyebrows went up, and he watched expectantly as Amethyst turned toward the door.

"Thanks, Mr. Whisperer," said Amethyst. "I'll help you bring them in. Ask him to bring us a dozen buckets of warm water next." She stopped at the door and looked back at the little unicorn. "The Secret Weapon needs a bath."

So began castle life for Amethyst. Though the material comforts were more than she could have dreamed of just a few short chapters earlier, she found it much like her old life on the farm. In fact, except for getting to eat anything she wanted at any time of day or night, having tons of beautiful clothes, bathing in warm water, getting paid in gold for what she loved to do anyway, sleeping in a bed with curtains and piles of pillows and comforters, being followed by a team of servants who jumped at the chance to make her every whim a reality, and living in a massive stone fortress with a garrison of precisely trained, heavily armed soldiers guarding the walls, it was exactly the same as her old life.

Oh, and not sneezing anymore.

Just as had happened before, Amethyst's allergic acrobatics had dwindled within a few hours of reuniting with Nova, first to a series of dainty little *choos!*—like the sneezes of a princess, or a kitten, or perhaps a princess's kitten—and then fading away altogether. This, more than anything else, gave Amethyst confidence that Nova had successfully reattached to her and that his recovery would be rapid and complete.

Though she found most of castle life quite pleasant, there were some things she found very hard to understand. For example, the first few times anyone had mentioned dinner, Amethyst had sung out, "If we're having any!" But no one had laughed. After five or six occurrences of this, Amethyst began to understand that certain topics that were considered hilarious in the surrounding countryside—like starvation, for example—might not be found funny at all inside the castle. Everyone there had a job to do, and those jobs usually didn't include laughter. Unfortunately, this seemed to hold true even for the Court Jester, who had appeared so saddled with chronic unhappiness that Amethyst had asked him if he suffered from depression.

"No," came the unsmiling reply, "I find I rather enjoy it."

During her second day at the castle, Amethyst was introduced to the Royal Offspring, Princess Gwyneth and Prince Todd, and their dog (not a Royal Offspring), a slobbery, jiggly-skinned bull mastiff named Bear.[††††] Though the prince and princess treated her with appropriate courtesy during the meeting, Amethyst found interacting with them somewhat awkward. She thought perhaps it was because her frame of reference as a girl two social classes below peasant made it impossible to identify with the imaginary problems of people who lived in castles. Either that or they were just spoiled. To Amethyst, Gwyneth and Todd seemed half asleep, almost wooden, and though they complained about

---

[††††] Short for "Barbearian."

everything—like the hardness of the poached eggs at breakfast, and the softness of their mattresses (Amethyst had needed them to explain to her what a mattress was), and being forbidden by their father from having a second dog[++++]—the possibility that they might do something to improve their situation had apparently never entered their minds.

Amethyst wasted no time in suggesting that what they most needed was something to shoot for in life, a purpose higher than themselves, a well-defined and regularly-reviewed schedule of Growth Goals.

"You should each get a personal organizer," she suggested. "You know what they say: if you fail to plan, you plan to fail."

Gwyneth and Todd thanked her with

---

[++++] Though it was seldom spoken about openly, the Royal Offspring had earned something of a reputation for causing more than their share of trouble. For example, they once caused a castle-wide panic when Barbearian had escaped through a hole in the outer wall and treated himself to a Royal Frolic by sneaking samples from the food tables at the open-air market in town (the salt-pork had proven to be his favorite). After scampering through the market with his tail between his legs and a string of sausages trailing from his mouth, the angry townspeople, pitchforks in hand, had chased the flabby bandit back to the iron bars of the castle's main—but decidedly closed—front entrance. Princess Gwyneth and Prince Todd, seeing their pet exhibiting an abnormally urgent desire to get inside the bars, had begun shouting "Barbearian's at the gate!" whereupon the Royal Guard, thinking the fortress under attack by foreign invaders, had launched the entire castle into combat mode.

appropriate politeness then walked off with Bear, complaining to each other about the length of the reading lessons from their personal tutors.

Strange as they were to her, Amethyst was better able to understand the children at the castle than some of the adults.

For example, Amethyst once approached Ro-bear while he was talking with a pair of soldiers who were standing guard outside a low, stone structure that was attached to the main castle.

"Hi, Robber," Amethyst said playfully.

"Please don't interrupt just now, Amethyst," said Ro-bear, looking in through the open door. "Weekly sand inspection, you know."

Amethyst looked into the room and saw that, indeed, it contained nothing but a large pile of sand. She opened her mouth to speak, but then remembered that Ro-bear had asked her not to interrupt.

"That will be fine, Soldier," said Ro-bear, pulling the door shut with a bang. He locked the door with a key, then looked cautiously around the courtyard before dropping the key into his pocket. Next he removed a small charcoal stick (Amethyst thought it looked suspiciously like a crayon) from his pocket and made a checkmark on a piece of parchment that was nailed to the door of the sand room. There were many, many other checkmarks already on the paper.

"Well done," Ro-bear said to the soldier. "Carry on." He turned and left the soldiers at attention on either side of the door. Amethyst hurried after him.

"Weekly sand inspection?" she asked as she caught up to him.

"That's right," he said. "That sand pile was inherited by King Engelbert from his father, King Archibald. Those soldiers are part of a platoon assigned to guard the sand, and every week I perform an inspection to make sure it is still there. That sand is reserved for a Very Special Purpose."

"Like what?" said Amethyst.

"Well," admitted Ro-bear, "I honestly don't know. I'm not sure *anyone* knows, anymore. But we do not need to know why we do our jobs in order to do them well."

"You don't?" she said.

"Nope. That's one of the things you learn when you become a grown-up."

"But," Amethyst said, "they're guarding dirt."

"Technically, it's sand" he said.

"But you're spending your lives guarding sand and you don't know why?"

*"I'm* not spending my life guarding sand," Ro-bear said, somewhat offended. *"I* just do the inspections—though sometimes I send my assistant to do them, but recently he seems to have disappeared."

"I'm sure he's hanging around somewhere," Amethyst said innocently.

"Regardless," said Ro-bear, "the point is

*they* are spending their lives guarding sand, not me."

"But there is sand all over the kingdom," said Amethyst. "Who would steal sand?"

"Shhhhhh," shushed Ro-bear, emphatically. He looked about, hoping no one in uniform had heard Amethyst's insensitive comment. "Okay. Look, what you say is true," he whispered. "No one is going to steal the sand. But that doesn't in any way diminish the importance of what those men are doing."

"It doesn't?" Amethyst was genuinely bewildered.

"No," said Ro-bear. "Nor should it decrease the satisfaction they get from their jobs."

"But doesn't it cost the king a lot of money to pay them?"

"Of course," Ro-bear said. "Good help is expensive. But what else can he do?"

She stood looking at him, utterly mystified.

"Try to understand," Ro-bear said, being careful to keep his voice low. "I know they aren't serving any useful function, but we can't fire them.§§§§ The people already blame the king for the high unemployment in the kingdom, and letting these men go would only make it worse. Besides, there are far more horrible ways to spend your life than guarding dirt no one is going to steal, even if you don't know why you're doing

---

§§§§ Fortunately, this sort of thing would never happen with government workers today.

163

it."

"Technically," Amethyst said slowly, "it's sand."

"Precisely!" said Ro-bear. "Now you're getting it."

"I'm not sure that's a good thing," she said.

Amethyst didn't know whether she should continue trying to understand what he was saying, or be afraid it might begin to make sense to her. She tried to imagine some extenuating circumstance, something she didn't know about that would make guarding dirt important in some way. She could not think of anything, but decided to say no more about it. He was the adult; she was a little girl. He was an officer of the Royal Court; she was a commoner two steps below "peasant." Besides, it was the age of fairytales, and she could see no harm in letting Ro-bear continue in his.

## Stuff at the Castle

Nova continued to improve as time passed. By the second day he was up and prancing circles around Amethyst as they had done in his first days at the farm. By the third day his whinny had returned to its old sparkles and wind-chimes self. It seemed to Amethyst that it was Nova's way of laughing, and she laughed along with him as he pranced. Whenever he let loose with one of his whinnies, the castle staff and townsfolk who were in the courtyard would look at each other with questioning eyes, wondering what strange secret could possibly be inside the high walls that surrounded Nova's yard. Then staff and peasant alike would watch the guarded door that led into Nova's grain building, dying to find out what sort of creature could make such a marvelous sound. But the only ones who ever came out were an eight-year-old girl and a very old man in a robe, and the people were pretty sure it wasn't one of them (though some weren't so sure about the old man). But no one asked Amethyst or the H.W. what was inside the building, for the king had made it clear that it was a Secret of Greatest Importance, and that no one was to speak of it.

After a week, Nova was once again the picture of health. His appetite had grown enormous. He was putting on weight nicely, and seemed to Amethyst to have grown a measure since she had first seen him standing among the strawberries. Nova watched Amethyst with a new look in his eye that communicated quite clearly that, horse-paradise though it was, he was ready to get out of his little walled yard.

Amethyst and her mother fell into something of a routine. Amethyst's mother filled the hours by cleaning things or wandering into the kitchen and attempting to help with the cooking. The castle staff regarded her with some suspicion, since she had appeared without explanation and, in an attempt to keep Nova a secret, was forbidden from telling anyone her real role at the castle. All the staff knew was that a middle-aged woman in a splendorous gown had suddenly taken to wandering about the castle and polishing random items with a tattered dress she seemed always to have in hand, or bursting unannounced into the kitchen and trying to get the Royal Chefs to add rhubarb to whatever they had going on the stove. It was not long before a rumor took root that she was actually the queen's long lost Albanian aunt, who had only recently been discovered living the life of a poor farm wife on the Road of Desolation a few miles from town. And as for her unusual behavior, most were convinced the rhubarb had something to do with it.

One day, Amethyst glanced into a side room as she moved down one of the castle's less-traveled corridors, and saw a suit of armor she recognized bending over a table covered with maps and drawings.

"Timmy!" she exclaimed. She ran into the room, arms open wide, but stopped just short of hugging him. There were several other people in the room and she didn't want a repeat of the poison sumac incident.

"Amethyst!" said Timmy, bending down and risking a hug anyway. "It's so good to see you!"

"I see you have worked your way up to going without your helmet," she said. "I'm very proud of you!"

"Don't be too impressed," he said. "We are, after all, indoors, and this place doesn't have a thatched roof. I'm afraid I still need it in some of the castle's larger rooms—and whenever there's a chandelier overhead."

"Hang in there, Timmy," Amethyst said with her trademark enthusiasm. "You'll get it."

The room contained several important-looking men and diagrams hanging on the walls and covering the tabletops (the diagrams, not the important-looking men). There were maps, charts, and drawings showing the movements of circles and "x"s with arrows pointing every-which-way. The south wall was papered with large sheets of parchment covered with scribbles from that morning's free association and brainstorming session.

"What is this place?" asked Amethyst.

"This is the Royal War Room," said

Timmy. "We've been simulating battles and conducting feasibility studies around the clock since we arrived."

"*This* is where you disappeared to?"

"Yes. Thanks to your encouragement and a glowing report from Mr. Flintlock about the forest rescue, they hired me as a consultant on battlefield strategy and warfare tactics"—he leaned in to whisper in her ear—"not to mention being paid a tidy sum to keep from telling what we know about a certain Secret Weapon that shall remain nameless—"

"We're sharing state secrets with little girls now, are we?" interrupted a man in a bearskin cape, his voice thick with scorn.

"Oh, this is no little girl, Duke Ellington," said Timmy, straightening to face the man. "This is the Keeper of the Official Secret Weapon of the Realm."

"Well, whoever she is, she's doing a whiz-bang job of impersonating a little girl."

"Well, I mean yes, she *is* a little girl," said Timmy, "but what I meant to say is, she's on our side. She's part of the team, one of us."

"We're recruiting children now? Pray tell, what's next? Drafting men-at-arms straight out of nursery schools? While we're at it, we might as well pick up an old hermit or two and hope for a unicorn to show up to lead us into battle!"

Timmy and Amethyst stared at him without moving, plastic smiles cemented on both their faces.

"We're going to war, for goodness sake!" continued the Duke. "Who's charged with taking notes today? Count Bassie, I want it entered in the record that the Strategy Consultant is giving state secrets to a scullery maid!"

"Noted, Duke Ellington," said a Noble who was scritching furiously with a quill in one corner.

"But she's cleared for all military secrets," said Timmy. "She's the Keeper of the Secret Weapon."

The Duke rolled his eyes.

"And what magnificent Secret Weapon has the king come up with this time?" he asked snidely.

"I'd tell you," said Timmy, taking Amethyst's hand and leading her out of the room, "but I'm afraid you're not cleared to know."

Amethyst walked next to Timmy as he clanked along. The hallway, which was paneled with dark hardwood and lined with tapestries, was deserted except for the two of them.

"We can speak more freely out here," he said.

"So we're really going to war, then?" Amethyst asked.

"I'm afraid so," Timmy replied. "King Engelbert sent Tarnation an official Challenge to Battle as soon as Nova came into his possession. Though they sent their acceptance immediately—it's a matter of national pride for them since they've won the last three battles—their reply didn't arrive back here until this morning."

"When will the battle be?" said Amethyst.

"Two weeks from today. The Tarnationals said they were ready to go immediately, but that we could have an extra week to build up our army."

"That was gracious of them," said Amethyst.

"They seemed to think so," said Timmy.

"Speaking of building up armies," said Amethyst, "what happened to Mr. Flintlock? He just disappeared without saying goodbye."

"When the queen offered to let you live here, Mr. Flintlock tried to slip quietly away. I think he wanted to avoid disrupting your big moment with a tearful goodbye. I suspect that, deep down, he's a good deal more sensitive than your average arms dealer. Before he left, the king offered him a job with the army, but he turned it down. Said he would have accepted it in his younger days, but he had to get back to running the Maul. He talked them into adding his name to the Royal List of Approved Suppliers, though, so you might see him around."

"I hope so," said Amethyst. "I never got a chance to thank him—or to give him the rhubarb I owe him."

For a moment, Timmy wondered if Gunter's secretive departure had less to do with avoiding a scene than avoiding rhubarb. He hoped not, but had to admit it might have been a factor.

"How's the Secret Weapon doing?" said Timmy.

"Oh, he's fine," said Amethyst. "Sprung back to his old self."

"That's good to hear." Timmy stopped walking and leaned in closer to Amethyst. "I'll tell you," he said, "and this is in the strictest confidence—I'm worried."

"About what?" said Amethyst.

"We got a report this morning from our spy in Tarnation. He says that, although he wasn't able to discover exactly what it is, he has confirmed that Tarnation has a Secret Weapon of their own, and that it is formidable."

"Four-midible?" Amethyst looked suddenly alarmed. "How many midibles do you think Nova is?"

"Formidable means strong or hard to beat," said Timmy, tousling her hair. "The king pretended it didn't bother him when we got the news, but I could tell he was as worried as I am."

"What if their Secret Weapon beats a baby you-know-what?" Amethyst asked urgently. "I don't want Nova to be hurt."

"Neither do I," said Timmy, "but I don't know what else we can do. An army led by a you-know-what is supposed to be unbeatable. We'll just have to trust that King Engelbert knows what he's doing."

Amethyst and Timmy looked blankly at each other, neither wanting to say what they were really thinking.

* * *

Gunter Flintlock crossed over the draw-bridge and entered through the castle gate, leading a pony that was pulling a cart loaded with neatly stacked armor. As he walked up the path toward the castle, the magical sound of a unicorn's whinny filled the air. Gunter did not look toward the high walls of Nova's yard, but only smiled knowingly and kept walking.

About the middle of the courtyard, he came upon a line of soldiers all dressed in battle armor, practicing their maneuvers in unison while a shorter suit of armor strode back and forth in front of them, shouting.

"Thrust, parry, collect, jab! Thrust, parry, collect, jab! That's terrible! My little sister could thrash the lot of you in open combat!"

Gunter thought there was something familiar about the voice coming from inside the leader's helmet.

"Excuse me," said Gunter. "Don't I know you?"

The suit of armor reached up and removed its helmet to reveal a head belonging to Scar the Thief[*****].

"I thought so!" said Gunter.

"What are *you* doing here?" she asked in surprise.

"Exchanging a load of chainmail for the big

---

[*****] Thought I was going to say "Timmy the Tremulous," didn't you?

172

battle," said Gunter. "My supplier goofed up the sizes on the last shipment. All in all, not an impressive showing for a fellow who has finally gotten on the Royal List of Approved Suppliers. But what about you? What happened with the Self-Actualized Persons and all that?"

"I gave it up," she said. "Turns out stealing uni—er, uh, *Secret Weapons*—from little girls just wasn't my thing. Besides, I couldn't take any more of Ralph's complaining, so One-Eye used his connections here at the castle to get me a job as a drill instructor for the army."

"Given your skills with a blade, lass," said Gunter, "I'd say the king made a good choice."

"That's kind of you to say," she said. Though he couldn't be sure, Gunter thought for a moment that Scar was actually blushing.

"I see you've lost weight," he said. "I approve."

"Thank you for noticing," she said. "Though there are easier ways to go about it, turns out hanging upside down in a tree for ten days is a marvelous weight reduction technique. It also gave me some time to reflect on my life, and cured my lower back problem as well."

"I'm so glad to hear it," said Gunter.

"Um," she began, obviously embarrassed, "I'm sorry about that whole thing in Nightmare Forest. I just wanted you to know it was nothing personal."

"Think nothing of it, lass," said Gunter graciously. "Different time, different enemies.

Besides," he said, winking slyly, "the lump on my forehead is almost completely gone."

They both chuckled awkwardly.

"You know," she said, "we're whipping the troops into shape for the upcoming battle with Tarnation. We could use an instructor with moves like yours. I could probably get the king to give you a teaching position."

"Ah, lass," he said, "thank you for the compliment, but I'm afraid I'm too old and slow to be of any use here. Besides, I'm awfully busy with the Chop-n-Maul. Business always picks up considerable before a war."

"I understand," she said, looking down at her armor-plated feet.

"I've been meaning to ask you," said Gunter, "what kind of name is 'Scar' for a dainty little thing like you, anyway?"

"It's short for 'Scarlet,'" she said, looking rather scarlet as she blushed. "My father was an artist, and named all of his children after his favorite colors."

"How...unusual," said Gunter.

"Yes, the other kids used to tease us about it growing up. That's why I shortened it to 'Scar.' Of course, it wasn't nearly as hard for me as it was for my brother, Chartreuse."

"Well, I don't think 'Scar' fits you so well," said Gunter. "From now on, I shall call you Scarlet."

"And I shall call you Gunter," she said.

"Agreed," he said. "Say, if you're done with

174

your weight loss program, how about we have supper together when you're done whipping the troops?"

She blushed again, harder.

"Why, Gunter," she said, "are you asking me on a date?"

"Well, I have a reputation as something of an armor expert," he said with a wink. "Did you know 'armor' is the French word for 'love'?"

"Why, Gunter," she said, covering a lilt of girlish giggling with her war gauntlet, "you rogue!"

# The Banquet

The night before the battle, King Engelbert threw the traditional Pre-Skirmish Banquet—though this one had been scaled back to more of a cocktail party/reception due to significant cost overruns on war preparations. At one end of the cavernous ballroom was a long table draped in beautiful linens covered with flatware, dishes, and napkins. In the center of the table was a magnificent ice sculpture of a *humongus magnolius* tree, carved to the last detail by Queen Arabella an hour beforehand (refrigeration hadn't been invented yet, so she'd had to be quick about it).

At the other end of the room a collection of non-union musicians (hired from the local *Going Baroque* franchise) were playing recorders and a lute, which is a kind of medieval guitar. Though the musicians were practiced with many popular songs of the day, everything they played sounded just like a song you might have heard called *Greensleeves*, largely because any song played on recorders and a lute sounds just like *Greensleeves*—even a Christmas carol like *What Child is This?*

King Engelbert and Queen Arabella milled about, plates in hand, talking with their guests. Aside from a dozen uniformed waiters who held forth trays of fancy finger food as they moved between the guests, nearly everyone in the room was a member of a Noble family. The exceptions to this were Amethyst, her mother, and the Hoarse Whisperer, who stood awkwardly by a punchbowl watching the ornately dressed Nobles ignore them.

The people in the room seemed light-hearted—perhaps too lighthearted, Amethyst thought. She could tell that several of them were worried about the next day's slaughter, and had been so for some time. To her, it seemed a dark cloud of dread had been gathering over them all—

"My, these dishes look familiar!" said Amethyst's mother, examining a plate she had picked up from the table. "Reminds me of the set your father and I got for our wedding, Amethyst."

At that moment, Timmy clanked up to them and snapped—a little too quickly—to a halt. He tipped precariously to one side for a second, then settled back to center.

"Gather round," he said in a low voice. "I have word on the final plan for tomorrow. The king has had a special wagon built, like a large wooden cage with a canvas cover over it. This way Nova can be transported in secret. At the battle, the wagon is to be pulled up in front of the entire army, and the cover removed, emboldening our men and striking terror into the hearts of the Tarnationals. Hopefully, that alone will be enough to send them running."

"And what if it isn't?" asked Amethyst. "What if they have something that can defeat even a magical un—"

"Careful, Amethyst!" exclaimed Queen

Arabella. She and the Royal Offspring had approached unnoticed while the little group was huddled around Timmy. "Loose lips sink ships, you know."

"Your Highness," said Amethyst, curtseying to each of the Royals. I was going to say 'you-know-what,' not, well, that other thing."

"Say, that's very good," said Amethyst's mother. "Rondolay is in possession of a magical uniwhat. It's like a secret code."

"Yes," said the queen. "So long as the secret code remains secret."

"Yes, Your Grace," said Amethyst. She noticed that the prince and princess each had a serious-looking man from the castle staff standing at attention behind them. "Princess Gwyneth. Prince Todd," she said. "Who are these men you have following you? Bodyguards?"

"These are our Personal Organizers," said Princess Gwyneth. "We wanted to show them to you since it was your idea that we should have them."

"Your personal organizers are human beings?"

"Yes," said Gwyneth, a touch of doubt creeping into her expression. "Aren't everybody's? That was what you meant, wasn't it?"

"Um...sure," said Amethyst, though she wasn't at all sure. "Of course that's what I meant. Either a full-grown man or a little paper booklet that you write things in...I mean, you know, whichever."

Just then, King Engelbert swept toward them with his Royal Robes flowing, arms spread in warm welcome.

"Ah, the maiden Amethyst and her colleagues!" he said. "How are my special agents tonight?"

"Fine, Your Highness," said Amethyst. "And how is our special king tonight?"

"Oh, I am very well, thank you. I am excited to see how our 'you-know-what' performs tomorrow—"

"Oh, he knows the code, too!" said Amethyst's mother excitedly.

Everyone in the group had grown used to her by now, and so ignored that she had just interrupted mid-sentence the reigning monarch of a small but not completely insignificant European nation.

"I see you have no food," continued the king. "Everyone, please, grab a plate. We're serving our state dish tonight, Chicken Rondolay. I can't stand the stuff, personally, so please do what you can to prevent any leftovers."

Amethyst sniffed the air. "Why am I smelling Christmas trees?" she asked innocently.

"Come stand next to me, Amethyst," the queen said quickly, exchanging eye rolls with her husband, who raised a hand and self-consciously smoothed his eyebrows.

"Trying out the pine sap again, huh Pop?" said Prince Todd, who was old enough to have known better but still young enough to feel like he could get away with saying such a thing. He would find out after the party that he was mistaken about that.

"Punch!" said Engelbert, suddenly very embarrassed. "I see you all need punch." He moved to the punch bowl and began slopping the red drink into small crystal cups, then passing them around.

"Your Highness?" asked Amethyst from the far side of the queen.

"Yes, my dear?" said the king, still slopping and passing.

"I'm told we have word from Tarnation that their Secret Weapon is three or four midibles."

"What?" said Engelbert, stopping mid-slop.

"Well, Sire, I was just wondering, how many midibles do you think Nov—um, I mean 'you-know-who' is?"

Engelbert looked at Amethyst for a moment before an expression of partial understanding dawned on his face. Though he never fully got that part about the midibles, his Royal Heart was touched by the fact that he was speaking to a poor, fatherless, farm waif, and that she was very worried about her pet unicorn.

"Oh, don't you worry about that," he said gently, lowering himself to one knee so he could look her in the eye. "I've had some of my best men working on that very question around the clock, and they have assured me that 'you-know-who' is at least eleven—and possibly even *twelve*—midibles, no doubt about it." He gave her a

180

knowing wink before struggling to his feet again.

For nearly an entire moment, King Engelbert, Monarch of Rondolay, had succeeded in reassuring a worried little girl. For the span of two breaths, she had believed him. After all, he was a grown-up. More than that, he was the ruler of a small, but not completely insignificant, European nation. She figured he should know what he was talking about even if he did smell more like a pine-scented air freshener than any man ever should. But that moment of hope, that feeling that maybe he wasn't as silly as he sometimes seemed, came to an abrupt end when the scrunching action of the king's wink caused one of his eyebrows to spring with an almost audible "doink" from his forehead and plunge like a furry Acapulcan cliff diver into his cup of punch.

## Departing for Battle

The day of battle came at last, and the castle was a convulsion of activity. The courtyard was full of soldiers running hither and thither, being shouted at by drill instructors, assembling into companies and squads and other malformed groups that were supposed to be companies and squads, which set off another run of drill instructor shouting, and so on. Wagons moved this way and that, being loaded and unloaded with such urgency that more than once they forgot to move the wagon to a new place between the loading and unloading parts. Children were running, women were saying tearful goodbyes to their husbands, and Queen Arabella was handing out cheese sandwiches in monogrammed lunch bags that she had calligraphied herself. Heathrow Payne observed the scene from horseback, scritching furiously on a pad of parchment with a charcoal stub. Through the middle of everything ran Barbarian the dog, frantically barking to warn the Royal Family that about a thousand strangers had suddenly appeared inside the castle walls.

Duke Ellington rode about on horseback. He watched with alternating satisfaction and irritation the successes and failures of the "soldiers" he had been assigned. I put the word "soldiers" in quotation marks because a wide majority of the men were not soldiers at all, but farmers and peasants who had been scrounged from the surrounding countryside and subjected to an intensive two weeks of military training. As he watched his men gather clumsily into clots of humanity every bit as disorganized as any other company or squad in the courtyard, it occurred to Duke Ellington that they might actually have been better at marching in formation *before* they had received their intensive two weeks of training.

"Looks like we're well on our way to yet another glorious military defeat for the Royal Kingdom of Rondolay," he muttered to himself. "We're nothing if not consistent, but I suppose there's naught to be done about it now."

King Engelbert was riding around on his favorite Arabian (horse, that is) giving orders to this group and that, and generally adding to the confusion wherever he went.

Duke Ellington supposed there was naught to be done about that, either.

The H.W. stood watch at the door outside Nova's yard, waiting for the arrival of Nova's secret transport wagon.

Inside the yard, Amethyst was dressed again in her red leather gnome armor. She stood next to Nova, combing his silky mane and gently stroking his soft nose.

"There, there," she said gently. "Everything is going to be all right." She thought for a moment, then added, "I hope."

Now that the day had actually arrived, Amethyst wished very much that there was some way out of the whole mess. She could tell Nova was nervous, too, because he seemed to be having trouble standing still. He kept raising his hooves and stamping them down again as if he was trying to climb a set of stairs that weren't there. Though Amethyst couldn't tell how much Nova understood of what was going on, it was clear he knew something was happening outside his high stone walls.

After the soldiers had been grouped, regrouped, and grouped again, Nova's wagon arrived, harnessed to two muscular and rust-colored draft horses driven by Timmy in his thoroughly polished suit of armor. He put the horses into reverse and gently backed the wagon up to Nova's building. In the back of the little wagon was a wooden cage covered entirely by cloth. Timmy climbed down from the driver's seat and helped the H.W. extend a burlap cover to make a little tunnel so Nova could walk up the loading ramp without being seen. When all was ready, Amethyst emerged from the building leading Nova by a halter. She walked him quickly up the ramp and into the cage in the back of the wagon.

The inside of the wagon was relatively nice by medieval standards, considering it was one of the first horse trailers in history.†††††  Its top cover

---

††††† After all, in a time when most of the population was absorbed with finding their next meal, who would have thought to build a wheeled vehicle for an animal that had four perfectly

was rough burlap through which came surprisingly little light. On the floor was a grain bucket and plenty of hay.

Then Amethyst noticed the latch on the door.

Now that I have specifically pointed out that Amethyst noticed the latch that would keep Nova imprisoned in the wagon, I'm sure that you are beginning to suspect what happened next, Dear Reader: that Amethyst in her desire to keep Nova out of the war was so crafty and so brave that she left the door to the cage carefully unlatched, and as a result, on the way to the battle, Nova burst gloriously from his cage, caught Amethyst and her mother on his back as they leapt from the driver's seat, and galloped like the wind away from the army, the War of Prodigious Length, the country of Rondolay, and pre-wilted rhubarb farming, and that they all escaped to a life of relative ease and prosperity giving unicorn rides to children on a beach in Hispaniola. I would love to give you all the details about those events, but I can't because...well...that isn't what happened. Though I'm sure you were clever enough to see all that coming, Amethyst, alas, was not. The truth is the thought of leaving the cage unlatched never even entered her mind. (Besides, such a neck-spraining plot twist would have violated the standards of realism and believability I've so consistently estab-

---

functional feet of its own? Why build a transportation device for a transportation device?

lished over the past 185 pages, don't you think?)

Anyway, before leaving Nova in the back of the horse wagon, Amethyst patted him on the side of the neck and said, "That's my good boy. It'll all be over soon." Then she went out and dutifully latched the door on the wooden cage. Timmy helped her pull the cover down and tie it in place—no easy task with gauntlets on one's hands.

At the front of the wagon, the H.W. was already settled on the driver's bench. King Engelbert, dressed in full battle armor, rode up as Timmy and Amethyst climbed up next to the H.W, followed by Amethyst's mother, dressed in full battle ball gown.

"Is the Secret Weapon all loaded, Amethyst?" said Engelbert.

"Yes, Your Highness," said Amethyst, looking down at the wagon's floorboards. Whatever happened in the next few hours, she knew things would be never be the same afterward.

"Dear woman," said Engelbert to Amethyst's mother. "There is no call for you to go with us into battle. You are to stay here with Queen Arabella and keep watch for our safe return."

"In your dreams," retorted Amethyst's mother.

"I beg your pardon?" said Engelbert, more surprised than angry, and more shocked than surprised.

"Let me put it this way," said Amethyst's

mother. "What kind of mother would I be letting my eight-year-old daughter go off to war without me? It's just not going to happen. King Engelbert, you have nigh on a thousand soldiers here who have so consistently failed to walk in a straight line when commanded that even now arriving at the battlefield with all of them remains in doubt. I've been watching them. Right now you have much bigger problems than whether or not an old farm wife rides with her daughter into one of your battles."

"Now I see where Amethyst gets it," muttered Engelbert. Still, he knew she was right; he had much more pressing worries staring him in the face. Without another word, he wheeled his horse sharply and rode off to a gaggle of trumpeters who were waiting next to the gate. The king gave them a command and the trumpeters played a blaring fanfare written especially for the occasion.

The army began moving, mostly toward the gate.

As they awaited their place in line, Amethyst spoke up again. "I've been wondering what Nova would think about being used as a weapon, secret or otherwise, in a battle where people actually intend to harm each other," she said. "I don't think he would like the idea very much."

"You-know-what's should never be part of an army," rasped the H.W., "because, as everyone knows, they belong in the *neigh*-vy." The joke, if I can call it that, didn't go over any better than any of his previous horse jokes. In fact, as incredible as it may sound, this one might actually have been worse.

"Thanks for trying to cheer me up, Mr. Whisperer," said Amethyst, on the edge of tears.

Timmy shook the reigns to start the wagon moving forward, and said, "But please, don't let it happen again."

Outside the castle gates, the town's main street was lined with peasants, street beggars, and everyone else who wasn't going to the big battle. This was about the closest the people of Rondolay ever got to seeing a modern parade because the Fourth of July hadn't been invented yet. Everyone cheered as the soldiers passed, and many pointed whenever a celebrity like the king or Heathrow Payne appeared. Some people— mostly women—waved their hankies or the dishrag part of their dresses, craning their necks to see if they could spot husband or brother or Uncle Ebenezer in the river of soldiers moving by.

Then Nova's cart emerged from the castle gate and rumbled dramatically across the wooden drawbridge.

"Oh, look!" said one peasant woman to another. "There's the little rhubarb girl. Why is she going off to battle?"

"I don't know," said the other, "but doesn't she look snappy in that little suit of armor? I wonder if she ever found her lost water buffalo?"

Rondolay's battlefield was a wide, flat expanse of ground not far from the Rondolay/Tarnation border. It was completely surrounded by trees—except for the side with the bleachers and refreshment stand—and King Engelbert had always liked it because it was well drained and had few gopher holes. Tarnation had a battlefield that would have served just as well, but this one, as was the custom in such situations, had been selected by tossing a coin when the Challenge to Battle had been accepted. Rondolay had won the toss, and so today would enjoy home battlefield advantage.

As the army of Rondolay filled in at one end of the field, Amethyst could see the army of Tarnation on the other side, just out of arrow range but close enough to shout to. They looked to her to have about the same number of men as Rondolay, though they seemed better organized.

Timmy stopped the wagon inside the clearing. "Looks like the pre-battle show has started already," he said, nodding toward the field where a giant man with tangled red hair and beard was running in circles, screaming like a lunatic, and performing the "hair razor" with his axe. "The king always hires Barthus the Berserker from the Rent-a-Rogue in hopes of intimidating Tarnation. It doesn't usually work, but the spectators appreciate a little entertainment while they're waiting for the battle to start."

Amethyst, her mother, and the H.W. climbed down from the wagon to wait for the army to re-sort and ready itself. Across the entire width of the field, Nobles and squad leaders were trying to organize their men. The sight did nothing to increase Amethyst's confidence.

"War wares!" came a familiar voice on the breeze. "Get yer last-minute battlefield accessories here! Buy now and get this lovely set of monogrammed daggers thrown in absolutely free!"

It was Gunter. He was standing on a wooden platform at a peddler's cart that was loaded with an impressive variety of blades, bows, battleaxes, and armor. A sign nailed to the front of the cart stated (except for Heathrow Payne's misspellings): *The Chop-n-Haul: Guaranteed to bring you through alive or your money back. Approved Supplier to the king.*

"Look, Mother," said Amethyst, "it's Mr. Flintlock! Is it okay if I go say hello?"

"Okay, dear," said Amethyst's mother. "But be sure you're back before the war starts."

"I will," said Amethyst, and ran off.

Gunter was just finishing up a transaction with a worried-looking soldier as Amethyst approached.

"...that sword is an excellent choice," Gunter was saying to the soldier. "And all sales today include free engraving of your name or initials on the item purchased."

"Say, I'd like that!" said the soldier.

"Though, if it's all the same to you," said Gunter, "we'll put off the engraving until *after* the battle."

The soldier, who had begun to relax a little with the sword in his hand, suddenly looked worried again as he thanked Gunter and walked away with his purchase.

"Mr. Flintlock!" Amethyst exclaimed as she ran up to him and wrapped him in a ferocious hug. "It's so good to see you!"

"Why, if it isn't my little Amethyst!" said Gunter, hugging her back and laughing. "How have you been, lassie?"

"Just fine, thank you. Mother and I have been living in the castle since we last saw you."

"And how has that been?"

"It's okay, though I'm really starting to miss eating rhubarb."

"Now there's a string of words I never expected to hear."

"Are you going to be in the battle, Mr. Flintlock?"

"Ah, lass, I would have gladly joined in when I was younger, but I'm afraid I'm too slow and frail now," he said, lifting a 200-pound anvil from the wagon, carrying it quickly to a nearby fire, and placing it gently on the ground.

Amethyst was surprised to see the thief formerly known as "Scar" kneeling at the fire, heating a badly chipped sword in one hand and holding a blacksmith's hammer in the other.

"What's *she* doing here?" asked Amethyst,

slightly alarmed.

"She's helping me out today," said Gunter. "There's nobody better with a forge hammer."

"But isn't she...you know...that potato thrower?"

"Well," said Gunter, measuring his words while unconsciously raising a hand to rub his forehead. "She was."

"But she isn't anymore?"

"Nope. Not anymore," he said.

"What happened?"

"Amethyst, do you know what the word 'armor' means in French?"

"Huh?"

"Oh never mind. Let's just say it's that old Flintlock magic."

"Oh. Okay." Amethyst really didn't understand, but she wanted to get back to Nova. "Well, I guess I'd better go."

"Okay, lass," said Gunter, calling after her as she ran off. "You be safe now, and take care of that you-know-what!"

Scarlet pulled the sword, sputtering and glowing bright orange (the sword, not Scarlet), from the fire and carried it to the anvil.

"Flintlock magic!" she said. "Mr. Gunter, you really are a rogue!"

"Not me," said Gunter, innocently. "I just own the Maul." He pointed toward the battlefield where Barthus was still performing, and said, "*He's* the rogue."

# *War!*

Amethyst returned to Nova's wagon, lifted a side flap, and peeked inside.

"How're you doing, boy?" she said.

Nova just looked at her without saying anything. She could tell he was worried, though she didn't know exactly how she knew. She thought it must have something to do with the soul connection thing they shared.

"I believe they're almost ready," came a voice like a rusty gate hinge.

Amethyst dropped the flap and turned to see her mother and the H.W. standing there.

"Oh, Mr. H.W., do you think it's true what they say? Do you think Nova can help us win?"

Just then a blaring fanfare filled the air from the king's hired trumpet section.

"Looks like we're about to find out," said the H.W., pointing toward the front of their army where two perfectly formed lines of cavalry stood. The lines were made up of every Noble in the kingdom, dressed in colorful battle armor and sitting motionless on their horses. In front of them, King Engelbert was riding out onto the field alone.

On the other side, King Fescue the Fearless of Tarnation rode out to meet Engelbert. When they came to the midpoint of the field, they halted their horses, removed their helmets, and began exchanging the customary courtesies.

"Hail, cousin Fescue!" Engelbert shouted grandly. He hoped it was loud enough for both armies to hear. "I'm gratified that you showed up on time—for once."

"Given Rondolay's record against Tarnation," returned Fescue[+++++] at the top of his voice, "I'm surprised you showed up at all."

"That is not the last surprise you will have today, I'm thinking," Engelbert shouted with all the confidence he was able to pretend he had.

"You are right," shouted Fescue, "for if you are thinking, then I am indeed surprised again."

The army of Tarnation burst into laughter and a supportive smattering of applause.

Engelbert had no response for that.

Fescue continued: "I should imagine that one of your advanced age would have thinner hair by now."

Engelbert had prepared for battle by gluing to his head the longest, thickest swatch of bear pelt in the Royal Hair Collection. He was hoping the look would provoke fear in his cousin at close quarters. Unfortunately, with the mass of com-

---

[+++++] Fescue was in fact the son of King Ficus the 14th, who had started the whole war mess with Engelbert's father, Archibald, at the First Battle of Humongus Magnolius. Fescue's father had been something of a rebel at heart, and had broken from the family tradition of naming their firstborn sons after houseplants, complaining that "Ficus" was a ridiculous and degrading name unbefitting a monarch, and so opted instead to name his heir after a species of yard grass that was particularly meaningful to him.

pletely black bear fur standing on end on top of his cousin's head, all that was provoked in Fescue were doubts about Engelbert's sanity and a vague urge to begin humming Christmas carols.

"A hairy man is a manly man, I always say," said Engelbert, attempting to casually run his fingers through the tufted mat. "'Tis a truth that I am most fortunate to have such thick, luxurious locks, though it does trouble me so to keep it combed!"

"Come now!" shouted Fescue. "Surely Rondolay has a competent taxidermist[§§§§§] who could help you with that."

Again the army of Tarnation laughed, this time with greater applause.

Again, Engelbert had nothing to say.

"Will you surrender now, Engelbert, or do you wish to wait until after we have destroyed your army?"

"There will be no surrender today!" shouted Engelbert, the strength in his voice surprising even him. "At least—I mean—not from us—for we have a Secret Weapon that makes us undefeatable!"

"Another of Rondolay's famous Secret Weapons!" shouted Fescue. "This should be

---

[§§§§§] A "taxidermist" is a person who stuffs animals after they are dead (for that is by far the safest time to stuff them). Though the armies were too far away to see it, Fescue's remark caused Engelbert to blush in embarrassment, for he actually had gotten the bear fur from the kingdom's Taxidermist Laureate back home.

good. I hope this one works out as well for us as did the Flaming Logs of Fate."

Engelbert did not shout this next part. He was done with being laughed at. In fact, as Engelbert looked back across his life, he found he was bone-tired of losing and feeling ridiculous, and had been so for a long, long time. He found Fescue's eyes with his own and held them there. Strangely, he was not worried. He was not afraid. He was just...plain...tired.

"You have never taken me seriously," he said so only Fescue could hear. Engelbert raised his helmet in both hands a pressed it firmly onto his head. "Well, cousin, you'll have to take me seriously now."

Slowly, Engelbert raised himself from his saddle until he stood tall and straight and regal in his stirrups. Then, with all the volume he could summon, he shouted, "Bring forth the Secret Weapon!"

All eyes turned back to Rondolay's front line where a wheeled cart rolled dramatically out onto the field, pulled by two draft horses. Timmy was alone at the reigns, but a squad of highly trained Rondolayan soldiers (they had been practicing this part for weeks) was jogging along behind. The wagon continued almost to the midpoint of the field before stopping. The squad of soldiers took their assigned positions on either side of the wagon, their expressions wooden.

"Ooooo," said Fescue in mock dread. "This must be the part where I'm supposed to go all jelly-legs and beg your mercy."

"Beg or don't," said Engelbert, sounding more kingly than at any previous moment in this story, "whichever you choose, but you will not win this day."

"Ah, cousin," said Fescue, putting his helmet on. "When will you learn that Rondolay is not the only country capable of producing Secret Weapons?" Fescue made a quick gesture behind himself with his hand, and the army of Tarnation split into two groups like Moses parting the Red Sea. In the gap that was formed, a huge war wagon, decorated with jagged, frightening-looking ironwork and armor, was pulled grandly onto the battlefield by eight draft horses. At each of the corners of the wagon, braziers of flaming coals sent up columns of smoke and fire. In the middle of the wagon, a red tarp that covered something large and intimidating was tied down along the sides and at each corner. Two squads of highly trained Tarnational soldiers (they had been practicing for months) jogged along behind. The war wagon came to a stop just short of midfield. The Tarnational soldiers moved into position, one squad on each side of the wagon, their expressions like steel.

King Engelbert was unimpressed by the display—almost. He remained standing in his stirrups and shouted: "Prepare to reveal the Secret Weapon!"

The squad of Rondolayan soldiers obediently cut the ties that held the cover on Nova's cart, took the edges of the cover in their hands, and waited.

King Fescue stood up in his stirrups. "Prepare for unveiling!" he ordered.

His men snapped to positions around their war carriage, each grasping an edge of its cover.

Back on the sidelines, Amethyst watched with her mother, the H.W., Gunter, and Scarlet. She reached up and silently took hold of her mother's hand on one side and the H.W.'s on the other. Gunter put a strong hand on Amethyst's shoulder.

"Have faith, lass," he said. "Anything can happen."

"Now!" screamed King Engelbert and King Fescue in unison.

At long last, the moment had come. The soldiers on both sides *pulled.* The covers came free of the wagons and fell, almost in slow motion, flapping gently downward and piling up into heaps on the ground.

A moment later, King Engelbert found himself flying through the air, spinning heels over head and completely out of control.

The people of the Middle Ages lived in a world that was very different from the one we live in today. Living in a primarily agricultural society, they were more likely to be farmers than any other profession. Even the ones who were tradesmen, such as blacksmiths or taxidermists, had large gardens at home from which they harvested the fruits (which were usually vegetables) of the land by the sweat of their brows.

To fully understand what happened at the 27th Battle of Humongus Magnolius, it is important that you remember two things:

The first thing you must remember is, as mentioned above, the soldiers in the army—the ones who weren't Nobles, that is—weren't really soldiers at all. They were peasants or farmers, commoners who would receive no reward from defeating the opposing army except for the relief of having made it through yet another battle without dying. This meant that neither army was particularly motivated to win. Even the members of the army who found military combat personally fulfilling were keenly aware that the good feelings brought about by having survived would be more easily achieved by simply running away. The two armies remained on the battlefield only because their kings commanded it, and that's before you take into account the fact that a thousand common farmers were being forced to stand close together in the hot sun in an age when most people bathed like clockwork—once in January and once in July (and the July bathing hadn't happened yet). I have told you all of this to make clear there were very few people on that battlefield who actually *wanted* to be there.

And the second thing you must remember, the thing more important at that moment than anything else I've just mentioned, is what horses do when they find themselves in the presence of a real unicorn.

We now rejoin our regularly scheduled war, already in progress.

It is a fact of history that when the Secret Weapons were revealed in the 27th Battle of Humongus Magnolius, there was not a living thing on either side, human or otherwise, that was not shocked beyond the capacity to speak.

Both armies were shocked to learn that the imaginary creatures known as "unicorns" were not imaginary at all.

The Nobles of Rondolay were shocked to realize that King Engelbert, for once, had come up with a Secret Weapon that wasn't so ridiculous that it would cause them to be laughed off the battlefield by the opposing army.

King Engelbert was shocked to realize that his army still had every chance of being soundly thrashed by the opposing army because Tarnation's Secret Weapon was, in fact, another white and nearly perfect unicorn that wasn't Nova.

Amethyst was shocked to see that Tarnation's unicorn would probably defeat whatever powers Nova's presence provided for Rondolay, if any, because Tarnation's unicorn was every bit as regal and competent-looking as Nova, but much larger and more powerful, projecting an impression of betterness that was quite possibly better than two times better than Nova's betterness.

And Nova, the lively, graceful, and nearly-perfect Secret Weapon of the Royal Kingdom of Rondolay, was shocked to see on the far side of the battlefield, in a cage very similar to the one he was in............his mother.

And all of the horses on both sides—draft, cavalry, farm, and otherwise—though thoroughly shocked (as far as horses are able to be) at finding themselves suddenly in the company of *pair* of unicorns, simply bowed.

"Look, Mother!" shouted Amethyst, pointing at the second unicorn in disbelief. "Oh, Mother, *look*!" Her eyes were enormous with surprise.

Amethyst's mother considered asking whether the larger creature was a unicorn or a rhinoceros—she was too far away to see its eye color—but decided to hold her tongue.

The uproar that next engulfed the battlefield was a shock to all in attendance, but none more so than the Nobles and the two kings, all of whom found themselves tumbling from their horses and colliding painfully with the ground.

After finding himself looking up into the sky from flat on his back, Duke Ellington jumped quickly to his feet and frantically tried to regain his composure, almost as though he meant to topple from his mount and crash clumsily into the dirt. His embarrassment, which was already extreme, worsened when the unbridled laughter of every last man in the armies of Rondolay and Tarnation reached his ears. He turned in anger toward the army to see who had dared laugh at him, and was surprised (and more than a little relieved) to see the answer was "No one."

The men in the army of Rondolay were craning their necks to get a look past him to the center of the battlefield at a sight possibly even stranger than seeing two mythological beasts at the same time.

At the sight of his mother, Nova released the loudest, longest whinny Amethyst had ever heard from him, though this one was more constricted, like it was being squeezed by alarm. When he had finished the whinny, he launched into a fury of bucking, thrashing about wildly in his cage.

Then Nova's mother whinnied, even louder than Nova had, but the sound that came from her contained something darker and more powerful than the sparkle-and-laughter whinnies Amethyst was used to. The larger unicorn was well beyond alarmed—she was *angry*—and the cry that came from her massive frame rolled outward and upward into the sky until it became something you or I would ordinarily have mistaken for thunder. Amethyst, having more experience with unicorn whinnying than anyone else there except the unicorns themselves, thought that if the sound were translated into human words, it would mean: "All right. Now you've done it. I'm finished fooling around."

The female unicorn did not buck or jump, but deliberately lined up her back end with the doorway of her cage, and fired off a kick that made a deafening clank and a shower of sparks from her metal shoes hitting the iron bars. It was an impressive effort, but the bars held firm.

Nova noticed what his mother was doing and stopped bucking. He then began kicking, too, aiming his smaller hooves at the wooden bars in the doorway of his cage.

"They're going to hurt themselves!" said Amethyst, running onto the battlefield. "We've got to help them!"

Gunter and Scarlet looked at each other. "We'll not have unicorns hurtin' themselves while I can do something about it," he said. "Are you with me?"

"I'm with you," she said, pulling a pair of red-hot swords from the forge.

They raced after Amethyst.

"Look!" shouted one of the Rondolayan soldiers, pointing to midfield. "A Royal Hairpiece malfunction!"

And it was perfectly true.

When Engelbert's horse had unexpectedly dropped to its front knees, his rump (the horse's, not the king's) had stayed high in the air. The king had instantly launched out of the saddle and turned a spectacularly ungraceful somersault down the length of his horse's neck. Engelbert's impact with the ground had knocked his helmet off, taking most of his unusually thick and luxurious Royal Hairpiece with it. The extra glob of tree sap glue he had applied that morning in preparation for battle had paid off—but only in the front. The remainder of the swath of bear hide had flopped over Engelbert's face like a black, hairy washcloth, completely eliminating his ability to see. ******

Though Engelbert realized that he was no longer on his horse, his stunned mind couldn't make sense of what had happened. He knew only that he was suddenly unable to see an enemy whom he believed was still on his horse and about to begin raining blows down on him. So he

_____

****** The soldiers, shocked at the sight of their usually well-groomed king with a mutinous hairpiece covering his face, turned and asked each other, "Did you know he wore a hairpiece?" at which the askee without exception replied, "Well, yeah, actually I did," to which the asker invariably nodded and admitted, "Yeah, me too."

did what any regal monarch in a medieval fairytale would do: he burst into a blind, screaming panic. He jumped to his feet and began swinging his sword in wild, unseeing circles while screaming for help from his army. As his fractured thoughts tried to comprehend how Tarnation's Secret Weapon had succeeded in extinguishing the sun, it did not immediately occur to him that he had bear fur in his eyes.

Though Engelbert's luck had been remarkably bad, his cousin's didn't turn out to be much better. When he hit the ground, Fescue's helmet was turned almost completely around, leaving him as blind as his now ridiculous-looking cousin. Fescue, hearing Engelbert's shouts and fearing an imminent attack, climbed to his feet and also began swinging.

Amethyst reached the back of Nova's wagon, unlatched the door, and swung it wide. "There you go, boy," she said breathlessly. "Now you're free."

Nova looked gratefully at her for a prolonged moment, then burst through the doorway onto the field.

Gunter and Scarlet headed right past Nova's cart toward the Tarnational war wagon, being sure to take a wide path around the sword-slinging monarchs. As he went by, Gunter noticed Fescue's helmet turned around backward.

"A good helmet liner will prevent that, you

know!" he yelled as he ran.

Fescue spun blindly around toward Gunter, sword raised in defense. "Who's there?!" he demanded. "Who said that?"

"He should have gotten that helmet from me!" Gunter shouted to Scarlet, who was running a ways ahead of him. "I give a free liner with the purchase of all headgear!"

Whether Fescue would have been helped by a helmet liner or not, it remained a fact that the two kings were completely unable to see and in an utter panic about the attack they each thought the other was about to deliver.

Engelbert brought his sword down where he was sure Fescue would be—but only succeeded in planting his weapon in the ground, where it stuck, buried halfway to the hilt. At this, Tarnation's army laughed uproariously.

Fescue, on the other hand, lifted his heavy broadsword too quickly above his head—and toppled over onto his back, sending Rondolay's army into an unrestrained explosion of guffaws.

At the same moment, Scarlet reached the Tarnationals, a squad of highly trained guards who had run out to confront her. The guards drew their swords and positioned themselves to form a half-circle wall between Scarlet and the Tarnational war wagon.

She stopped in front of them and held up her swords, which were still glowing and sputtering sparks. "Okay, boys," she said menacingly. "Who wants to go first?"

"Blymy," said one of the guards in utter amazement. "It's a girl!"

"And a dwarf!" said another guard, pointing to where Gunter was approaching at full speed.

For the barest instant, Gunter seemed to stumble as he ran, but the stumble changed immediately into a perfectly performed cartwheel, which turned into a powerfully executed handspring, which launched him higher into the air than you would have believed if you hadn't just seen it with your own eyes. The Tarnational guards watched open-mouthed as the armored dwarf sailed over their heads, landing on the back of the lead horse harnessed to Nova's mother's wagon. From there, Gunter continued his acrobatics, flipping and springing from one horse to another until he landed on top of the cage in the back of the wagon. He dismounted to the ground with a half-twist flying flip, landing solidly on his feet behind the wagon.

He looked up to find himself half-surrounded by the second squad of unicorn guards, glaring savagely with swords drawn.

"Prepare to meet your maker, dwarf," said the Captain of the Guard, stepping toward Gunter.

"How many times must I tell people?" said Gunter. He reached out and calmly placed his hand on the pin in the latch that held shut the door to the great iron cage. "Don't...call...me...

DWARF!"

Gunter pulled the pin.

The one guard who was not flattened when the massive unicorn came blasting from its cage like a four-legged freight train on its way to save its baby, looked wide-eyed at Gunter, then at the other members of his squad lying on the ground (the ones still in the area, that is), and ran away.

Meanwhile, Engelbert was tugging mightily at his sword, which was still embedded in the ground. At last, Engelbert combined all his strength into a single, titanic *heave* on the broadsword, which released from the ground so suddenly that it might have been flung from his hands and sailed across the battlefield if he had not been clever enough to intercept its trajectory with his chin, knocking himself to the ground where he lay nearly unconscious.

Again, Tarnation's army roared with laughter.

Meanwhile, Fescue was frantically engaged in what might be described as a combination of crawling and stumbling. He was trying desperately to climb back to his feet in full battle armor, an activity which is a pretty funny thing to see even when the one trying to get up doesn't have his helmet on backward and isn't surrounded by bowing horses and two armies in the iron grip of hysterical laughter.

Then Engelbert, who had managed to stand despite the wooziness from hitting himself in the chin, tripped over his horse's head and fell flat.

More laughter filled the space between the armies.

And so it continued. First Engelbert would swing wildly and miss—and the Tarnationals would laugh.

Then Fescue would flail comically with his face still wedged into the back of his helmet, and the Rondolayans would roar with mirth.

This went on for several minutes, each side laughing at the other side's king. But then Amethyst noticed that something was changing.

The two kings continued turning frantic circles, swinging wildly, shouting, and—most of all—*missing* each other. But after a while, when one of the kings made a ridiculous move, no matter whose king he was, *both* sides would laugh.

The sight was more than many of the soldiers could take. Some were doubled over with laughter, holding their ribs, tears streaming down their faces. Others, including two of the Nobles, had dropped to their knees, and were rocking back and forth gasping for breath between howls of laughter.

At last, with their strength nearly spent, each king began shouting threats at the top of his lungs and spinning wildly with sword outstretched, looking like a pair of blades that had just worked themselves loose from electric blenders. Then they fell one last time, and lay where they landed, panting in exhaustion, both too tired to get back up again. They had each failed to hit the other even a single time.

And still the armies laughed.

The scene had already broken by three minutes the Rondolayan record for Lengthiest Laugh at a Military Function, and was well on its way to becoming the funniest event in the history of all of Europe, when the laughter faltered and suddenly died away completely.

The men of the armies of Rondolay and Tarnation had stopped laughing when they noticed the two unicorns—one large and powerful, the other small and slight by comparison—had run to each other at the very center of the battlefield, and were nuzzling and neck-hugging each other as if they were a mother and son who hadn't seen each other for many pages. Nova's mother whinnied her greetings, and Nova turned a series of excited circles and whinnied in reply before his mother enfolded him in another neck-hug.

The armies watched the two unicorns, transfixed.

"Awwwwww," said Amethyst.

"Awwwwww," said the sweaty men in the two armies.

Amethyst's mother put her arm around the Hoarse Whisperer's shoulders and said, "Now isn't that just the sweetest thing you ever saw?"

The H.W. did not reply. He was trying to decide whether to wipe a tear from his eye or go on pretending it wasn't there.

Feeling slightly rejuvenated after his period of collapse, Engelbert smoothed his hairpiece back into its proper place, then struggled to his feet. Fescue was already standing, holding his helmet under one arm and squeezing the end of his nose with his fingers as if he were trying to coax it back into its previous Royal Shape. He forgot about his sculpting when he saw Engelbert stand up.

"Where did you get that unicorn?" demanded Fescue, his voice thick with anger.

"I could ask you the same question," replied Engelbert, gradually regaining his breath.

"One of our military patrols found her on the Tarnation side of the Plains of Eratosthenes," said Fescue, "not that it is any of *your* business."

The two kings watched the noble forehorns nuzzling and turning circles together.

"They seem to know each other," said Engelbert.

"I was thinking the same thing," said Fescue. "One of my men reported seeing our unicorn with a foal just before they captured her. You stole that little one from Tarnation!"

"We did no such thing!" said Engelbert. "I stole him from a little gir—er, I mean we found him wandering in a strawberry patch well inside Rondolay!"

"You are lying!" said Fescue. "Return the unicorn or prepare to fight!"

211

"That's what I came here for!" said Engelbert. "The fighting part, I mean."

Fire flashed in their eyes as the two kings readied their swords again and began circling each other as mortal enemies. Slowly, the two men moved forward to strike—

"You know," interrupted a small but insistent voice, "it would be a shame to hack each other to pieces after this tender scene."

The Royal Cousins looked confused for a moment, then lowered their swords and looked around.

There was a young girl in gnome armor standing beside them.

"I'm sorry," said Fescue. "What was that again?"

"I said," repeated Amethyst, "that it would be a shame to kill each other to pieces after this tender scene."

As Amethyst stood there, Nova and his mother trotted up behind and took positions on either side of her, in case she needed their protection. The two 'corns stood with Amethyst, staring steadily at Engelbert and Fescue. Though you may not know it from personal experience, unicorns are skilled at communicating a variety of feelings with their eyes. In this case, the unicorns communicated that they believed Engelbert and Fescue were behaving ridiculously.

Then the two kings became aware that they weren't being watched only by a little girl and two beasts, but by everyone in the two surrounding armies as well.

"You know," said Fescue, suddenly becoming self-conscious, "the child makes a good point. The mood just isn't right anymore."

Engelbert felt it, too. "Maybe another day then, cousin?" he said.

Then Amethyst spoke again, her voice unusually firm: "Why don't you both just stop?"

Fescue looked Amethyst up and down. "Cousin Engelbert, is she part of your army?"

"Well," said Engelbert, suddenly embarrassed at having an eight-year-old girl in his army, "I wouldn't put it exactly that way. But yes, she's one of ours."

"Rather a bold little urchin, isn't she?" said Fescue.

Engelbert shook his head in resignation: "You have no idea."

"What was that about stopping, child?" said Fescue. "Stop what?"

"Stop the war."

"Stop the war?" said Engelbert, shocked. "Until when?"

"Until forever," said Amethyst.

It took a moment for Engelbert to comprehend what she was saying. "I understand how you feel, Amethyst," he said, "but one does not simply stop a war."

"Why not?" Amethyst crossed her arms and watched them. It was clear she expected an answer and that she was prepared to wait as long as it took to get one.

"Um, well," said Engelbert, "because one just doesn't. We have a lot invested in this war. We've built an army, made all these uniforms...and just think how it would hurt your friend Gunter's business if we stopped."

Amethyst shouted to Gunter, who, with Scarlet, was watching the festivities from the top of the Tarnational war wagon. "Hey, Mr. Flintlock! Would it be okay with you if these two guys stopped the war?"

Gunter appeared to think for a moment, then yelled back, "I can't see where it would bother me any, lassie!"

Amethyst turned back to the kings.

"Grumpy—er, Gunter says it's okay with him."

"You see what I mean?" said Engelbert to Fescue. "I can't do a thing with her."

Engelbert became aware at this point that the soldiers, who had come to suspect that the battle had been canceled, had been creeping slowly toward centerfield. As they approached, the two armies joined at the edges into a single mass of thoroughly armed men, completely surrounding the kings, the unicorns, and Amethyst.

"Let me try," said King Fescue. "King Engelbert is right, child. We can't just stop the war."

"Why not?" repeated Amethyst. "It's not like your goal is to liberate people or stop a tyrant or defend home and hearth."

King Fescue looked nervously at the thousands of men creeping closer. A murmur had begun spreading through the crowd, and now it grew in volume.

"It's...," Fescue actually seemed to deflate a little, "...complex. I would explain it to you, but you wouldn't understand."

"I see what you mean," said Amethyst. "I am awfully young, and I have experienced much in the past weeks that I did not understand."

King Fescue's face blossomed into a smile. "You are wise to recognize your limitations, child." He said it like a teacher who has finally gotten through to a particularly dense student. "You see, Engelbert? All you need is to be clear about which of you is the child and which is the dictator."

"But," continued Amethyst, "these soldiers are much older and less limited than I. Perhaps you can explain it to them?"

Fescue's smile evaporated. The crowd got a notch louder and a step closer. Someone in back shouted, "Yeah! How about you explain it to us?"

"Look," said Amethyst, "each of your Royal Selves believes that having a unicorn will make your army unbeatable, *but you both have unicorns now.* If neither side can be beaten, then neither side can win. *The war will go on forever.*"

"The girl is right!" came another shout from the crowd. "Why don't you two knock it off?"

*"Besides,"* continued Amethyst, *"my*

215

*mother told me the Tree of Greatest Contention was struck by lightening and burned to a pile of cinders five years ago.* You are fighting over a tree that doesn't even exist anymore!"

Fescue looked shocked. "It did?"

King Engelbert nodded sheepishly. "I'm afraid so."

"I hadn't heard about that," said Fescue. "Haven't been out there since my father stopped boundary riding. That does put a different spin on things, doesn't it?"

"And she's right," said Engelbert, "we could never defeat each other, since each army has a unicorn."

"Yes," said Fescue. "She mentioned that already." He scowled and rubbed his chin as though he were deep in thought, though he continued to watch the approaching soldiers from the corner of his eye. After several moments he kicked at a small rock in resignation. "Oh, all right," he said at last. "Who am I to keep a war going when even the arms dealers want to stop?"

"Agreed," said Engelbert. He held out his hand as a gesture of peace to his cousin.

Shaking hands with a Rondolayan was a new idea to Fescue, and he was eying the offered hand warily when—

"Amethyst?"

Amethyst looked around at the circle of soldiers. One soldier had pushed out of the crowd into the circle and was standing staring at

216

her. He was wearing Tarnational armor and holding a wooden milking pail in one hand. He lifted his helmet visor.

"Amethyst, is that you?"

"Daddy?"

"Amethyst!" He dropped the bucket.

"Daddy!" she screamed as she ran to him, fell into his arms, and covered him in kisses. Then she burst into tears of joy and relief.

"*Move it, boys!*" came a shout from behind as the soldiers parted and a slight woman in full battle ball gown plowed through like a determined water buffalo. She joined the family hug, where it soon became impossible to tell whose tears were whose.

"Well, I guess that's it then," said Engelbert, raising his sword and pointing it skyward. "I declare the War of Prodigious Length officially over!"

"Uh, me too!" shouted Fescue, hastily lifting his sword overhead.

The crowd responded with a great cheer of approval which lasted a long time. When it had died down, someone from the back shouted, "But who won?"

Engelbert looked thoughtful for a moment, smiled, and nodded toward Amethyst. "I think she did," he said.

"Oh, Daddy!" said Amethyst. "Where have you been all this time?"

"Well," he said, "as you no-doubt guessed, I got misdirected on my way to the barn. I aimed myself in the direction where I thought the house was, and set off. But after a few hours it became obvious I had gone the wrong way.

"I wandered for a couple of days with nothing to eat, and I must have crossed the border because the first people I came upon were part of a Tarnational Guard unit. They thought I was a spy, and put me in prison for a couple of months until they were convinced I didn't know anything of value. Then they made me serve in the army until I could work off the food I had eaten while in prison. The trouble was I still needed to eat while I was in the army, and army pay isn't very much, so my pay never caught up to the amount they said I owed. A few months ago, I was made the Assistant to the Keeper of the Official Secret Weapon of Tarnation. It seems I have a knack for connecting with unicorns."

"Boy have *we* got a lot to talk about!" said Amethyst, laughing and hugging him again. "It will be so good to have you home at last!"

Amethyst's father hesitated. He looked at Fescue warily. "Well, Amethyst, that sounds wonderful, but I may not be able to go with you. I'm afraid I'm still part of the army of Tarnation."

"Please," said Fescue, mounting his horse (who, along with all the other horses, had stopped kneeling well before this). "Go ahead." Fescue turned back to Engelbert and explained, "That guy gets lost more than any soldier I've ever seen. We have wasted more man-hours searching for him than any sane monarch would believe. We

218

put him in the unicorn unit because that squad doesn't carry weapons. With his poor sense of direction, we were afraid to let him have a sword; thought he might get turned around in the heat of battle and begin attacking us."

"Really?" said Amethyst's father. "I can go?"

"You have to go," said Fescue. "No way you're coming back to Tarnation with us."

Amethyst and her parents gave up a mighty cheer, then hugged one more time. Then her father approached King Engelbert.

"I have great news, Your Highness," said Amethyst's father, putting his arm around Engelbert's shoulders and giving him a friendly squeeze. "Unicorns just love rhubarb. Did you know that?"

That glorious day was always remembered—for as long as it was remembered at all—as *The Half-Battle of Humongus Magnolius,* and it pretty much wraps up our story. But before I get to the "Happily Ever After," there are some things you might like to know about what happened to everybody afterward.

Following the half-battle, the soldiers from the two armies went home to their wives and children with the joyful news that the war was over and that they would therefore not be needed at the 28*th Battle of Humongous Magnolius* the following year.

King Engelbert returned to his castle where he made a lengthy speech from the castle wall that can be summed up as follows: "Since it seems we were fighting over a pile of cinders, anyway, my cousin King Fescue the First and I have agreed to split the pile down the middle, each take our half of the ashes back to our people, claim victory, and declare the war over."†††††† ††††††

---

†††††† In Rondolay, the cinders were carried carefully back to the castle, where it was decided they would be permanently housed in a Special Display in the castle's History of the Realm wing. They were stored under a glass cover with a beautifully calligraphied sign, hand lettered by Queen Arabella herself, stating: "The Spoils of War: These are the ashes of the Tree of

Since thousands of people had witnessed the Royal Hairpiece malfunction, King Engelbert gave up trying to hide his baldness. He donated his collection of animal pelt hairpieces to the History Museum, but they were never displayed publicly because they were mistakenly destroyed by a Royal Exterminator who had been called to service the room where they were stored. Though some of his subjects actually did make fun of Engelbert's baldness, it was far fewer than used to make fun of his vanity and ridiculous hairpieces,

---

Greatest Contention, won through the bravery of the men of Rondolay in the War of Prodigious Length." The compact heap of wood cinders remained on display for over a hundred years until a near-sighted castle janitor knocked into it with a broom handle, shattering the glass cover. The janitor, a conscientious but illiterate fellow who had never heard about the tree, the war, or King Engelbert, promptly swept the Spoils of War—glass shards, ashes, and all—into a nearby trashcan. Two weeks passed before anyone noticed that the Spoils were missing, at which point the problem of having a sign and no Spoils was effectively resolved by taking down the sign (it was last seen gathering dust in the "Retro" section of one of the kingdom's more obscure antique shops).

****** The glass cover was made from sand imported at great expense from a beach in Italy. At first, there was some discussion among the palace officials of using the sand that was stored under lock-and-key in the small room in the castle, but one official was adamant that the sand in that room had been put aside for a Very Special Purpose, and that, although he couldn't remember what the purpose was, he was pretty sure that melting it into a glass cover for the museum wasn't it. Besides, they argued, filling out the proper paperwork to requisition the sand from the guards would take so much time and effort that it would probably be more efficient to simply import sand from a foreign nation.

and he figured in the end it was better to be made fun of for something he couldn't do anything about than for a silly behavior that he was choosing himself. His new motto became "A bald man is a manly man," and when he caught Duke Ellington making fun of his baldness in front of the Nobles, Engelbert surprised everyone by laughing along.

Queen Arabella was relieved the war had ended. She found King Engelbert much easier to live with when he wasn't worrying himself sick about being humiliated at the next Battle of Humongous Whatever-us. With the end of the war, she even found time to take up needlepoint, glass blowing, blacksmithing, and macramé.

The Royal Offspring continued to live in the castle, and, on rare occasions, do things. I'm not going to tell you what they did, however, because this story is still not about them.

Barbarian the dog spent the remainder of his days escaping from the castle, causing panics and general mayhem, and gorging his fat self on stolen food. He would have told you he enjoyed it all immensely, if such a thing were possible for a dog.

The paparazzi continued to be annoying, and they still are to this day.

When Clawed the cat finally noticed that Amethyst's father had returned, he (the cat, not Amethyst's father) gave a yawning, drawn-out "yeoow" as if to say, "What? You again?" Beyond that, he didn't do anything. Ever.

Massey Fergusson continued looking and acting younger and younger while living in the stall next to Nova. He continued pulling a plow well past the age at which most horses are able, then Amethyst's father put him out to pasture where he (the horse, not Amethyst's father) spent the remainder of his days in a peaceful and fulfilling retirement. The mule that replaced him was named John Deere.

After another couple of years of frustration in Rondolay, Ralph Hood went to visit his cousin in England to study leadership techniques. He was immediately captured by the Sheriff of Nottingham, who, mistaking him for Robin Hood, handed Ralph over to Prince John the Usurper. Robin Hood began to plan a rescue, but thought better of it when he considered the advantages of having the authorities believe he had already been captured. Besides, he reasoned, Ralph was a really annoying guy. Ralph spent the years until King Richard's return attempting to convince his jailors that he was not his more famous (and far more dishonest) cousin.

One-Eye got a job as the target in the rotten vegetable throwing attraction at a traveling carnival. He was eventually hit in the eye by an unusually accurate potato thrower. "Curse the luck!" exclaimed One-Eye. "Blinded by unrestrained pottage!" At that point he moved his eye patch to his newly-injured eye, looked around with his previously covered eye and said, "Good thing I've always kept this one in reserve!"

Scarlet took a job working for Gunter, and they remained close always. They may have gotten married at some point, but you'll never know for sure unless this story sells enough copies to have a sequel.

Ro-bear spent the next several years writing a book called *The Philosophy of Efficient Government*. Heathrow Payne helped him, and it was eleven-thousand pages long when finished. For some reason, no one—not even Heathrow—wanted to publish it. So Ro-bear had the government print it. It didn't sell well, even when he gave it away for free, and the surplus copies were stored for years afterward in a locked room next to a large pile of sand.

Timmy the Tremulous took a position as a Royal Mine Inspector, and subsequently excelled working in the confined tunnels underground. Though he and Amethyst had more adventures together, Timmy—who has since asked to be called "Tim"—worked in the mines for years, where he has yet to be hit by a boulder from space.

The Hoarse Whisperer disappeared shortly after the half-battle, though Amethyst, Timmy, Gunter, and the H.W.'s laundry lady all knew where he had gone. They would occasionally drop by to see the old hermit, making sure to use the Member's Entrance to bypass the Cogs of Doom. The H.W. always pretended to be upset by the interruption, and would grouse about the rudeness of people bothering a simple hermit unannounced and circumventing his security system and didn't they know how expensive it was to have the Cogs installed in the first place? The others never believed he was truly angry, though. They would invariably remind him that, if he really wanted to be left alone, all he had to do was lock the Member's Entrance door. But he never did.

Gunter converted a corner of his shop to selling unicorn memorabilia since the war was over and unicorns had become all the rage in the kingdom.

Amethyst went with her mother, father, and Nova, back to live at the family farm where they immediately attached a rope to the house for her father to tie around his waist whenever he went outdoors at night. Amethyst's father became the *Keeper of the Official Rhubarb of the Realm* for both the kingdoms of Rondolay and Tarnation. He and Amethyst's mother made a pile of money from their farm (since rhubarb was now nearly as popular in leading cultural circles as unicorns), achieving Amethyst's life goal and landing the entire family squarely in the "peasant" social class.

Amethyst's mother used the family's mounting wealth to fulfill every dream she'd ever had, which is to say she bought three new dresses so she would have a different dishrag for each meal of the day. In gratitude for her brief service as the *Mother of the Keeper of the Official Secret Weapon of the Realm*, King Engelbert saw to it that her dishes were returned to her along with a *Certificate of Appreciation* hand lettered by the queen. Aside from that, and having her husband at home, life didn't change much for Amethyst's mother—and she always hoped it wouldn't.

Amethyst was hailed as a heroine for stopping the war, and was elevated well above the status of "peasant" in the hearts and minds of her countrymen. Her fame eventually spread to the point that she would often receive visits from people she didn't even know. Sometimes the visitors were paparazzi or publicity hounds; sometimes they wanted to meet the heroine of such an inspiring story; and sometimes they showed up with one of her fliers in hand, wanting to know if the spinning wheel was still for sale. But her favorite visitors always remained Gunter, the Hoarse Whisperer, Timmy the Tremulous, and, sometimes, Ro-bear—as long as it wasn't tax day.

You'll be relieved to know that—as of this writing—Amethyst remains allergy free.

And Nova, the competent and nearly perfect unicorn, stayed with Amethyst and her family, though he was free to go romp and play with his mother in Tarnation whenever he wished, which was often. But he always returned to his tiny stall in the little barn on Amethyst's farm, where a pail full of fresh strawberries would be waiting for him. He and his soul mate Amethyst lived out their days in relative peace and health, playing in the meadows, watching the sun set, and living happily ever after.

Until, that is, the day Amethyst's mother found an enchanted frog in the butter churn.

*The End*

## BLOOPER #1

Two armies face each other across a wide, steeply-sloped, and exceedingly muddy battlefield. The Army of Tarnation is spread along the top of the ridge, throwing rocks and leftovers from the food wagon down onto a line of Rondolayan soldiers who are using ten-foot poles to lever a massive, flaming log up the incline.

"I don't care what the king says," groans an overweight Rondolayan soldier to the skinny man next to him, "I'm pretty sure we're doing this wrong."

"You may be right," says Skinny, gritting his teeth and straining desperately at his pike to keep the whole caboodle from rolling back down on him. "This was much easier in training."

"In training, the blooming log wasn't on fire," says the fat one.

"And we didn't have anyone raining rancid porridge shot-puts down upon us," says Skinny.

Just then a cantaloupe a month past its sell-by date comes arcing in from above. The squishy melon hits Skinny square in the forehead, instantly engulfing him above the shoulders like a stinking, head-eating cannonball. He drops his pole in alarm to check that his head is still there.

A voice off-scene shouts, "Skinny! Pick up your pike! Quick!"

But it's already too late. Without Skinny's support, the Flaming Log of Fate stalls in its course, hesitates briefly, and begins to roll back down the hill.

The off-scene voice, now quite shrill, shrieks: *"FOR THE LOVE OF ENGELBERT, RUN FOR YOUR LIVES!"*

The Rondolayan soldiers break ranks and run downhill as fast as the mud and their leg armor will allow while the fiery tree trunk bounces after them like a demented, blazing steamroller.

At the top of the ridge, the Tarnationals stop throwing things long enough to erupt into laughter and wild cheering.

Halfway down the hill, two mud-covered figures work themselves free from the earth, leaving behind a pair of man-shaped impressions in the ground—one fat, the other skinny with a head like a cantaloupe.

Both men sit up, and the fat figure says through a layer of mud: "I told you it was a bad idea answering an ad for 'Expendable Soldiers.'"

## BLOOPER #2

The scene opens in the Royal Banquet Hall during the Pre-Skirmish Banquet.

King Engelbert sweeps toward them with his Royal Robes flowing, arms spread in warm welcome.

"Ah, the maiden Amethyst and her colleagues!" he says. "How are my special agents tonight—"

Suddenly, Barbearian the dog confronts Engelbert, barking furiously (the dog, not the king).

Engelbert's hairpiece vibrates for a moment and then jumps to its feet, revealing itself to be a terrified squirrel with its back arched, tail bristling, and claws clutching desperately at Engelbert's scalp. Engelbert's eyes fly open in shock as he screams in panic.

The squirrel leaps from his head and scampers off-scene with Barbearian lumbering after in hot pursuit.

The other characters in the scene explode into laughter.

Engelbert shouts, "What kind of lunatic writes a squirrel into a story involving simulated hair? I thought the thing was a prop! It was just lying there curled up next to the other hair pieces!" Then he leans forward so the union nurse can inspect the top of his head. "Am I bleeding?" he pleads. "Please tell me I'm not bleeding!"


## BLOOPER #3

Two men hooded in monk robes stand at

the entrance to the Hoarse Whisperer's cave.

"I hope we aren't late for the meeting," says one.

"Yes," the other says grandly, "let us proceed with all possible haste."

They approach the Cogs of Doom and step quickly onto the narrow plank bridge. They make it twenty-two feet before the one in front trips over the hem of his robe and falls forward, catching himself before falling flat.

"Watch out, you fool," says the other, looking doubtfully down into the darkness beneath them. "There's no telling how far down this thing goes."

"Yes," said the first, "good thing I caught this wooden lever to break my fall." As he is giving the lever a series of sharp up and down yanks to show how lucky he was, a huge razor blade flashes from a slot in the wall and slices the tip of his hood off. He freezes and asks, "What was that?"

"I'm not sure," says his companion slowly, "just be grateful you aren't any taller."

The men exchange glances of growing alarm as all around them the Cogs of Doom launch into terrifying motion.

*"DON'T JUST STAND THERE!"* shrieks an off-scene voice, *"RUN FOR YOUR LIVES!"*

The two men bolt in panic for the entrance, climbing over each other while spinning blades flash around and past them, shredding their hoods and robes as thoroughly as if they had been dropped into the bottom of an electric blender. They make it to the entrance, and tumble out onto the ground, eyes bulging in fear.

After a moment, the skinny one's expression changes to puzzled fascination as he looks at his friend. "Your left eyebrow is missing," he says.

The fat one raises one hand to check the place where his eyebrow had recently been, and says, "I told you it was a bad idea answering an ad for 'Expendable Hermits.'"

## BLOOPER #4

*"The next morning, Amethyst rose with the sun and hurried to tend the animals. It seemed to her that Petunia produced less milk than in recent days. If the decrease continued they would soon be back to measuring her output by the blatherly flingschlagel"*—Oh, sorry! Sorry everybody! I made another typo. Put Amethyst back into the house and reset the scene; let's try it again from the top.

## BLOOPER #5

Princess Gwyneth and Prince Todd are looking over the top of the castle wall, shouting "Barbarian's at the gate!"

The castle launches into a panic, everyone running this way and that, opening the armory, taking up sword and shield, and causing general pandemonium.

The head guard opens the door in the castle gate and looks out to see a sea of thousands of dirty men holding pitchforks and torches and roaring like an angry mob. "Wait a minute! Stop!" he shouts at them. "Stop, I said!"

The mob continues to shout, and the front gate begins to buckle inward as the men push forward to take the castle.

"SILENCE!" shouts the guard.

The men stop pushing as the roar of the mob dies rapidly to an awkward silence.

"This is all wrong," the guard says angrily. "It's supposed to be the dog, Barbearian, not an invading hoard! There's been a mistake! You men go home!" He slams the little door in the gate and does not reappear, though the men in the front of the mob hear him inside the wall shouting, "Who sent out a casting call for real barbarians?"

A fat barbarian turns to his skinny friend and says, "I bet they won't even pay us. I told you it was a bad idea answering an ad for 'Expendable Barbarians.'"

# DELETED CHAPTER

## On the Methods and Manners of Arms Dealers

This could get a little messy. It might be better to skip this chapter altogether. In fact, I think I will.

## AUTHOR INTERVIEW

The scene opens on two men standing in a cinderblock corridor in a public school. One of them is holding a toilet plunger.

INTERVIEWER: We caught author David Franklin, plunger in hand, at his day job as a janitor for the public school system in Montgomery County, Maryland. Mr. Franklin, we were hoping for a chance to talk to you a bit concerning *The Unicorn's Tale.* Didn't you get the message that we were coming?

*FRANKLIN: I'm so sorry. I know we were scheduled for two o'clock, but we've just had an overflow in the teacher's lounge, and they're really needing this plunger about now.*

INTERVIEWER: Just a few minutes, then?

FRANKLIN: *I guess it'll be okay. I've already turned off the water.*

INTERVIEWER: Hey, thanks so much. So, what was it like writing *The Unicorn's Tale?*

FRANKLIN: *It was great.*

INTERVIEWER (after a long, uncomfortable pause): Can you elaborate a bit on that?

FRANKLIN: *Well, they say never work with animals or children, so naturally I took on both at the same time. My wife thought I was crazy, but I just had to be a part of creating this story. I mean, what's not to like? It's got unicorns and a poor, sneezy little girl, and mean people hanging upside down in trees, a self-deprecating arms dealer, cliff diving eyebrows and Cogs of Doom, for goodness sake! I was thrilled when I heard we had the budget for actual Cogs of Doom. I was sure we were going to have to use computer generated Cogs. And throughout the entire story you have the relentless certainty that everyone except the Bad Guys will be wealthier, wiser, and deliriously joyful by the end.*

INTERVIEWER: Did you ever consider a sad ending?

*FRANKLIN: We did. For a while I was seriously considering a much sadder, alternate ending. We even had it all sketched out. But then I said to myself, "What are you doing, you maniac? You're breaking the First Two Unbreakable Laws of Storytelling!"*

INTERVIEWER: And what are those?

*FRANKLIN: The two rules are: 1) Always, always, always have a happy ending, and 2) When you're tempted to have a sad ending, see rule number one.*

INTERVIEWER: What was it like working with an actual unicorn?

*FRANKLIN: We were so lucky to get Nova for this project—he's been in so many fairytales, and real unicorns are so hard to come by. Nova had just finished a TV movie for Disney when we approached his agent about the Tale. I think he would tell you that once he heard about the project, he just couldn't say no. I mean here we were wanting him to play himself in his own life story. But I think the thing that really sealed the deal was when he found out rhubarb was involved.*

INTERVIEWER: I've heard he does his own stunts.

FRANKLIN: *Well, he wanted to, but we just couldn't risk it—I mean, do you know how lucky we were to have a real unicorn on the payroll? The union just wouldn't allow it. So we got this rhinoceros named Sam that we used as Nova's stunt double for the hazardous work, like for some of the battle scenes at the end. We got a couple of purple contact lenses from the prop department, and it worked great. Even Nova's mother had trouble telling them apart.*

INTERVIEWER: What's he like in person?

FRANKLIN: *Who, Sam? Well, he's always eating and he's kind of smelly, actually—*

INTERVIEWER: No, you fool! Nova! What's it like working with Nova?

FRANKLIN: *Oh, he's great. Fame hasn't affected him at all.*

INTERVIEWER: And what about Amethyst? This was her first fairytale, right?

FRANKLIN: *Amethyst was a treasure. She couldn't have been more perfect. It's almost as though she were created just for this part.*

INTERVIEWER: Well we certainly enjoyed experiencing her adventures with her.

*FRANKLIN: I'm glad to hear it. That's why I wrote the book in the first place. Now if you'll excuse me, I have to go plunge something.*

## ALTERNATE ENDING

The little unicorn woke with a start and shook his short mane to clear his head. He was lying under an archway of brush his mother had made near the edge of the forest.

"Mother!" he whinnied excitedly. "I've just had the strangest dream! There was a human girl who fed me strawberries and something called "rhubarb," and I got taken by some grumpy people and sold to a king with no hair! And I even had a horn!"

But the clearing in front of his cozy nest made no reply.

"Mother?"

The only answer was the breeze hushing lightly through the trees above and shifting the dapples of sunlight that decorated the forest floor.

He rolled from under the brush and looked around, but his mother was nowhere in sight.

The little unicorn was alone.

There had been times in the recently passed past that finding himself apart from his mother would have frightened the little white foal, but he'd had a growth spurt the previous week and now believed himself far too mature for such a juvenile response. Besides, he was too hungry at the moment to put much energy into being afraid.

"Those strawberries in my dream sure looked tasty," he thought.

Noting the distinct lack of berries in the vicinity, he reasoned that if his mother thought him old enough to leave alone, he must surely be old enough to go in search of strawberries.

"I'll probably be back before she returns," he thought. "Besides, what's the worst that could possibly happen?" The little unicorn hadn't yet learned how the craziest of ideas can seem like the most reasonable thing in the world from the safety of one's own home, especially if one's own mother isn't there to keep telling one how crazy one's idea is. As a result, leaving the clearing seemed a very good idea to him, and the little unicorn set off with the abandon of youth, and succeeded, almost immediately, in becoming hopelessly lost.

The alarm he felt at finding himself lost diminished considerably when at length he wandered into a thick patch of wild strawberries. He gobbled the berries in a manner his mother would not have approved of, and whinnied in gluttonous joy—a delightful mixture of horse and wind chimes and children laughing.

He dipped his head for another nip at an especially luscious berry plant that was right next to a tree stump. When he came back up, he was surprised to see a young girl approaching with a basket dangling from her arm. She held his gaze with a child's wonder, and he liked her at once. He whinnied again, this time with some sparkles thrown in, to tell her so.

The girl smiled at him warmly, then broke forth in the strangest whinny the little unicorn had ever heard:

*"AAAAAAAAAAAAA-CHOOOOO!!!!"*

Made in the USA
Middletown, DE
30 April 2024